A DCI Parrish C

The Embleton Murders

Bear Lawrence

Copyright © 2024 Bear Lawrence

The right of Bear Lawrence to be identified as the author of this work has been asserted by him in accordance with the Copyright, Designs and Patents Act of 1988.

All rights reserved. No part of this publication may be reproduced, stored in a retrieval system, or transmitted, in any form, or by any means (electronic, mechanical, photocopying, recording or otherwise) without the prior written permission of the author. Any person who does any unauthorized act in relation to this publication may be subject to criminal prosecution and civil claims for damages.

This is a work of fiction. Any names, characters, businesses, events or incidents, are fictitious. Any resemblance to actual persons, living or dead, or actual events is purely coincidental.

I would like to offer my sincere gratitude to

Kevin H. Hilton, Sam Burnell, Alex Stephenson and Liz.

Kevin is an author and co-author on the novel 'Admissions'. He has helped with cover design, not least by taking the photograph of Dunstanburgh Castle used for the cover. He also worked diligently to edit the manuscript.

Sam is an author and my mentor. She has been very kind and generous in sharing her knowledge, experience and time supporting me. Thank you for the cover design help too.

Alex is a retired murder detective. He most helpfully shared operational knowledge of murder investigations in the UK. He said, 'it might be exciting on the TV or in a book, but in real life, it's very dull.'

Liz, my other half, is my best friend and supportive of my writing efforts. She has also helped with reading and editing the manuscript.

Abbreviations & Explanations

CID – Criminal Investigation Department

DCI – Detective Chief Inspector

DI – Detective Inspector

DS – Detective Sergeant

DC – Detective Constable

FLO – Family Liaison Officer

SOCO – Scenes of Crime Officer

misper – missing person

BMI – Body Mass Index

IC-one – White, Northern European

post mortem – known as an autopsy in the US

per annum – for each year

CPS – Crown Prosecution Service

HMRC – His Majesty's Revenue and Customs, the US equivalent is the Internal Revenue Service (IRS)

ASAP, HQ, ID, etc. – if you don't know these, then this may not be the book for you. Google is your friend.

Chapter 1 – Dunstanburgh Castle

Devon Clarke held the hood of her long, quilted, royal blue coat firmly against her head. She wrapped her other arm around herself to keep her slim figure warm from the gusts of the cold salty wind, whipping inland from over the grey North Sea. Leaning against the wind, she picked her way carefully along the rough costal footpath that led from her home in Embleton to Dunstanburgh Castle where she worked.

The castle could be accurately dated back to the 1300's. Archaeological finds at the site indicated that this area was inhabited from as early as the Iron Age, between 1200 BC and 600 BC, when it was probably an ancient fortification. These days the remains of the castle were in the care of English Heritage, Devon Clarke's employer. She was the local manager, responsible for a handful of staff. All of them were in turn responsible for the safety of the public who visited the castle ruins.

Devon was a Virgo and the oldest pupil in her school year. The combination of her birthday and genes, meant she was the tallest girl in her year and taller than many of the boys. Standing out from the crowd was something she hated. Desperate to fit in, she was prone to exaggeration and a comfortable liar.

As a young girl, she was also quite chubby and despite her height was teased and bullied by her classmates for her height, weight and deceitful nature. The bullying had a profound effect on her and she developed an eating disorder as a teenager.

Now, she was an attractive thirty-year old woman, although she struggled to see that with her body image problems. Her big brown eyes sat in an oval face of smooth skin, above a thin nose and broad mouth. Her hair was naturally dark brown in large curls, which she kept at shoulder length. Despite being a pretty woman, she found it difficult to meet men due to her low self-esteem. It was also her low self-esteem that led to her poor choice of men who dominated her and put her down.

Her life often fluctuated between taking care with her diet and zealously attending the gym, losing weight and gaining confidence, until she had a boyfriend. Then she would enjoy meals, snacks and cosy nights in, choosing to watch movies over going to the gym, with the inevitable consequence that she gained weight. These disgusting men that she let into her life would then bully her and shame her about her size and shape. They would cheat on her and leave her for another woman. Devon would be heartbroken and devastated, only to repeat the cycle by hitting the gym again.

One might imagine she would be empathetic to others when she had power over them. Perversely, it was quite the opposite, Devon was controlling and a bully. She enjoyed the power bestowed on her as a manager at the castle and her staff suffered as a result.

She liked to arrive early at the castle to feel prepared and in control. As it was Saturday, it might be a busy day and she felt it particularly important to be well prepared. *Although possibly not busy today*, she thought, given the biting wind, which may deter visitors. As she approached the castle, Devon took a glance up as she always did to see if anything looked out of the ordinary from a distance.

Nothing looked out of place at the castle, but she noticed that there were quite a few gulls about, which was slightly unusual given the windy conditions. Head down again, she continued on towards the castle. The noise of the gulls squawking intensified to a crescendo as she approached where they were flocking out of sight from her on the jagged rocks below the cliff. As she scurried on by, the noise of the gulls started to diminish.

When she arrived at the castle, Devon began her strict morning routine. She took out her heavy bunch of keys and began opening the various doors and gates around the castle. As she passed between each of these, she made inspections of the property, fire extinguishers, emergency lighting and the like, to ensure all was well and safe for the staff and visitors who may be coming that day.

As she went about her business, she noticed her staff, Ian and Laura, walking towards the castle along the costal path from Craster to the south. The castle was remote and realistically accessible only by foot on two pathways. From Craster to the south and from Embleton to the north, the route she had followed. Devon despised the friendship between Ian and Laura because she felt excluded from it, blind to her behaviour being the cause of her exclusion.

When Laura and Ian arrived, Devon made sure she was there to ostensibly greet them in a friendly manner with a broad smile. Then, she briefed them in detail on what they would be doing that day. Her continuous micro-management riled all her staff.

Afterwards, the activity of the gulls was playing on her mind as she went about her work. She had walked that coastal path, hundreds if not thousands of times and it was unusual to see so many gulls concentrated in one area. The few times she had seen such behaviour was due to them feeding on the carcass of a large fish, or even a seal, washed up on the shore. If it was something interesting, such as a giant squid or a whale, it might make the local news. This would draw curious crowds to the locality and business would likely be busy at the castle.

Curiosity got the better of Devon. She pointed out the gulls to both Laura and then Ian. With Laura now watching the main gate, Devon was free to take a closer look at the gull activity.

Soon, Devon was at the cliff edge overlooking the area where the gulls were concentrated below. She could make out the shape of something on the rocks that the gulls were eating. But she couldn't quite make out what it was. *Perhaps a large seal or a porpoise?* she thought.

It was impossible to descend the cliffs here to take a closer look. She considered walking along to where it was possible to make her way down and then traverse back along the rocky shoreline. But it would take time and it would be dangerous over the slippery rocks in this wind. Instead, she took her phone from her pocket and took a photo.

She magnified the image but it wasn't clear what it was the gulls were feeding on. After wiping the camera lens clean, she zoomed in to where the gulls were and then took another photo. Again, she enlarged the image she had just captured.

Devon let out a blood-curdling scream. She dropped her phone, staggered backwards, bent over and vomited. The gulls were feasting on the corpse of a dead woman.

* * *

Later that day, DS Heather Ash pushed the witness statement across the desk towards Devon Clarke who was sat opposite her.

'Sign and date, here and here, please.'

Devon signed and dated the witness statement. In doing so, she recorded her version of the events that morning, at and around Dunstanburgh Castle. Prone to deceit and exaggeration, would it be her undoing?

Chapter 2 – DCI Parrish

Retired Detective Chief Inspector Parrish lay awake in his bed. He was in pain, utterly exhausted and grumpy. But it wasn't the pain and fatigue which was making him grumpy, it was the sound of his phone vibrating on the phone charger downstairs in the living room of his cottage.

Who was trying to contact him at this hour? he wondered, with more than a hint of consternation. His family and few remaining friends knew not to bother him before 10 am, if they wanted to escape his wrath. He reasoned it was probably junk-email, some scam or that car buying company still determined to purchase his BMW 6 series coupe he sold three years ago.

Curiosity got the better of Parrish when the phone vibrated again a couple of minutes later. He slowly rolled on to his side then swung his legs over the edge of the bed. He used the momentum of his legs to help him swing his body upright like a human pendulum. Every movement was a struggle and economy of movement was paramount.

It was wintertime and the old stone cottage was cold first thing on a morning. On the floor lay the clothes he had worn yesterday. Grabbing a t-shirt and fleece first, he sought to shelter from the chill. Then he eased his aching legs into some tired jogging bottoms that he wore around the house, wincing from the pain as he bent his hips and knees.

Parrish could barely remember his old life before ME/CFS and fibromyalgia. Life was now a never-ending mix of fatigue and pain with a whole host of other symptoms. Prescription medication helped knock the edge off the worst of the pain, most of the time. A concoction of vitamins, supplements and shop bought medication eased the pain in his joints and symptoms of IBS. But it was the brain fog that really troubled him.

As a young man he had joined the Metropolitan Police force in London. Hard-working, observational, insightful and intelligent, he had quickly risen through the ranks and joined CID. His stock continued to rise and solving some of the most serious and difficult murder cases raised his profile both in and beyond the Met. Consequently, DCI Parrish had become well known amongst the criminal, legal and detective fraternities in the UK and beyond.

Understandably, it was a stressful career with long hours, which had cost him his marriage. Later, when he contracted a viral infection in his late thirties he never recovered. He was forever exhausted, which he initially put down to recovering from his time in bed with the viral infection. However, he began to notice other symptoms such as unusual and unexplained pains in his joints and muscles, which came and went mysteriously.

But it was the cognitive difficulties that necessitated his early retirement on medical grounds. His concentration span was minimal and his memory unreliable. He found it extremely frustrating to know that he had a broad vocabulary, yet some days he was at a loss for words.

Eventually, Parrish was diagnosed with ME, Myalgic Encephalomyelitis, also known as Chronic Fatigue Syndrome. Under the Equality Act (2010) his GP found him disabled. Later, the Police Chief Medical Officer agreed and his early retirement at thirty-nine years of age was granted.

In the months that followed his retirement, he hoped he would recover. A previously effervescent man, full of life and used to working hard for long hours, he tried to push himself through the fatigue. But nothing worked, if anything he had regressed. His plan to pick and choose interesting and difficult to solve murder cases from the many police forces around the UK and abroad requesting his help, could not be realised.

Over the next couple of years, he learnt as much as he could about ME. Learning that there was no cure, was very difficult for him to accept. Depression overcast him like a black cloud. His GP referred him for a psychological assessment and he was found to have severe low mood and moderate anxiety. Counselling was recommended, which he reluctantly accepted. The counselling proved almost entirely futile. Each session involved an assessment of Parrish's depression and anxiety. Although these fluctuated, there was no material difference over the course of treatment.

Crucially, the counselling wasn't entirely useless in the longer term. Parrish had learned techniques to reduce his anxiety. These included no longer wearing a watch. Like many police officers, he had loved wearing large, expensive Swiss watches. He recognised that these were macho displays of wealth and status, a concept he didn't like, but he craved wearing them nevertheless.

Before long, he came to love the freedom of not watching the time, not being tied to deadlines and urgency. Parrish began to see such expensive watches as shackles, the wearer a prisoner to a money-rich and time-poor lifestyle. He knew that convicts released with a tag around their ankle sometimes wore the tag with pride, boasting of their criminal activity. He saw these watches as little more than tags boasting of a lifestyle that put work and money before friends and family. As he had unfortunately done himself.

The other trick he had learned from counselling was to unglue himself from his phone. Now, he often put it in a drawer or left it in another room. Gradually, he lost the need to check it constantly and he returned to the real world.

However, the vibrating phone downstairs had caught his attention. Slowly, he descended his uneven stairs which creaked under the heavy weight of his six-foot tall, broad-frame. He grasped the banister and wall for support to relieve pressure on his aching joints in his legs, which creaked in sympathy with the stair treads.

The first notification that had disturbed Parrish was an email offering another new price for his BMW - delete! The second was a text from an old friend, Professor Robbie Mustoe who was as typically efficient in his prose as he had always been.

It's been far too long since we last saw each other. It would be great to catch up soon, maybe over dinner?

DCI Parrish knew that Robbie was a very busy man with his successful academic career. Although Parrish was no longer a busy man, he didn't want his morning routine of breakfast and meds interrupted despite his eagerness to speak to his friend.

His routine had started forty-five minutes earlier. After waking, he had taken lansoprazole, which he had to take thirty to sixty minutes before eating. Now downstairs in his kitchen, he took a puff of his asthma inhaler. His eyes followed the rectangle of the kitchen cupboard doors to reinforce his breathing technique of; breathe out, hold, breathe in a puff of the inhaler, hold, breathe out again.

Next, he placed into a little ramekin; a multi-vitamin tablet, supplements of magnesium and turmeric, an anti-histamine, then prescription medication of allopurinol, lisinopril and naproxen. This part of his routine he finished with another puff of his inhaler.

Then he filled a large glass with blackcurrant cordial and cold water. After grabbing a muesli bar from a cupboard, he headed for his ox-blood leather Chesterfield recliner and heavy wooden coffee table in the living room of his cottage.

Once sat, he opened and ate the muesli bar first. Afterwards, he took each tablet in turn and swallowed each down with a gulp of cold blackcurrant. With all the tablets swallowed, he drank the remainder of the glass.

He pondered briefly why he had to finish the drink. He knew it was because one of the tablets demanded to be taken with a large glass of water, but brain fog prevented him recalling which one it was. Regardless, drinking plenty of liquid would be good for him.

The next part of his morning routine depended on what his day might involve. Mostly, he had a small, rich coffee from his pod machine. But he was reluctant to drink too much caffeine with his tendency towards high blood pressure. If he thought he might be having coffee later, he would abstain at breakfast time. With the possible prospect of seeing Robbie, he passed on the coffee. With his breakfast and meds routine complete, he sent a brief text to his old friend asking,

Can you speak?

Within a minute, Parrish's phone vibrated in his pocket.

In a meeting, will ring you after the hour.

Parrish looked at the time on his phone and saw that it was 9:15 am. He decided to take a shower as he had enough time before Robbie would call after 10 am. Slowly, Parrish climbed the stairs to complete his preparations for another day.

Freshly showered and dressed for the day, Parrish descended the stairs more easily as he was in less pain than earlier. A warm shower usually eased his joints and the naproxen had kicked in. Picking up his phone from the coffee table, he thought he could see that he had a message. With his reading glasses perched on the end of his nose, he saw that it was his medication app requiring him to confirm the meds he had taken that morning.

It was 9:50 am. Still feeling a little sluggish and having now decided it was unlikely he would see Robbie today, Parrish decided to have a coffee before the phone call. Perhaps old-fashioned in his ways, he thought it rude when people drank whilst having a phone conversation.

Still prone to thinking like a detective, Parrish reasoned that Robbie would ring no earlier than 10:05 am if the meeting was in his office. If it were elsewhere in the building, it would be 10:10 am to 10:15 am. If the meeting was somewhere else on the university campus, it could be anything up to 11:00 am.

'Ring of Fire' by Johnny Cash played on his phone. When he picked it up, Parrish could see it was bang on 10 am and Robbie was calling. Luckily, Parrish had just finished his coffee.

'Robbie!' an excited Parrish chirped.

'Scratcher!' an equally enthusiastic Professor Mustoe replied.

'It's been a while since I heard that old nickname.'

'Still riding motorbikes?'

'Well sort of. Scooters these days. Easier to get on and off. It was getting a bit difficult to swing a leg over the 750 Honda.'

Parrish had been a mad-keen biker from his teens. Riding a motorcycle fast is called 'scratching'. This comes from parts of the motorcycle and riders clothing and boots being scratched away by the road when leaning over in a bend. A famous motorcycle racer at the time was called Steve Parrish, teammate of World Champion, Barry Sheene. Little wonder that young Parrish had been given the nickname 'Scratcher' by his friends.

Robbie and Parrish had been friends since they were teenagers. They had met at sixth form college and struck up a firm friendship. After sixth form, Parrish had moved to London to join the Met and Robbie had gone to Edmonton University, also in London, to study Engineering.

They had regularly socialised over the next three years until Robbie finished his undergraduate degree and moved back north to Corbridge University to take a Masters degree. After completing his Masters, he stayed at Corbridge working as a researcher and completing a PhD part-time. After Corbridge University, Robbie became a lecturer at Embleton University, where his career had progressed to senior lecturer, reader and finally professor.

Historically, Embleton was a village housing, supplying and servicing the needs of the local agricultural and fishing workers and industries. Evidence exists of a church at Embleton dating from the late 1100's or early 1200's. The same site became the Church of the Holy Trinity, with links to Merton College of Oxford University from the 1800's.

A vicar of the church in the early 1900's, was dismayed at the uneducated locals with low moral standards and was determined to improve matters. This coincided with changes in local governance throughout the country with more power devolved to local parishes. The opportunity presented itself for the creation of Embleton University.

A campus was built to the south of Embleton, which itself became a bustling town. The building of the campus increased the size of the population, housing and services were expanded to accommodate these workers and the academics, administrators, technical and service staff that would follow.

Shops, supermarkets, gyms, a cinema and the HQ for Northumberland and Cheviots Police Force were all built there over time. Travel to and from this remote quarter of North East England was facilitated by the A1 main road and railway lines running between Edinburgh and London. A new trunk road linked Embleton and the campus to the A1 and Embleton was supported by the railway station at nearby Christon Bank.

The two old friends chatted for half an hour. Robbie was due to attend an engineering conference in Tadcaster the following week. Rather than head back north to home in Embleton, the pair agreed that Robbie would visit Parrish in Helmsley and stay the night. That would give them ample opportunity to catch up over a meal.

Parrish sensed that there was more to this planned reunion than Robbie had mentioned. 'Is there something in particular that you wanted to see me about?' he asked.

Parrish could hear Robbie smirking when he replied. 'Nothing gets past you Scratcher, does it? Yes, I do have something to run by you that has been bothering me.'

'Anything you want to tell me in advance, so that I can get the old cogs whirring in advance of next week?'

'Google the deaths of a Dr John Carlang and a Natasha Horseman. Both worked at Embleton University.'

'Mmm, interesting. Anything else, you want to prime me with?'

'Not really. It's a rather long story and strictly confidential. All I will say at this point is that I don't believe in coincidences.'

'Neither do I.'

After a short pause, Parrish couldn't help himself ask another question. 'The meeting you were at Robbie. Where was it?'

'At home.'

'At home?'

'Yes, it was a zoom meeting. Why do you ask?'

'No reason. See you next week.'

'See you then.'

Parrish ended the call and rubbed his chin ruefully. He hadn't worked since before the pandemic. He had heard of zoom meetings but had never taken part in one. The world had changed. He had expected a physical meeting, not a virtual one. Clearly, he needed to get up to speed with modern life if he was to solve a murder enquiry. *A murder enquiry? Why had he jumped to that conclusion already?* He smiled when he recognised that he missed the buzz of a case.

Chapter 3 – Dr Carlang & Natasha Horseman

Sat on his recliner with his old laptop across his knees, Google quickly brought up several news reports of the deaths of both Dr John Carlang and Natasha Horseman. Embleton University had also posted obituaries for both of them on the university website.

The same image of Dr Carlang appeared in the university obituary and in some of the news reports. He was smiling in his picture and was clearly overweight. Parrish considered the more correct term might be 'obese'. That would have to be confirmed by his BMI from his height and weight, which were measurable and therefore factual. DCI Parrish liked facts.

Dr Carlang was a Geography Lecturer at Embleton University. His obituary spoke of a '*dedicated academic with a remarkable career*'. The obituary in truth said very little other than to make pleasant words of a supposedly sadly missed colleague. To Parrish, the lack of discernible achievements in the obituary spoke volumes about Dr Carlang, his role, his career and lack of work-ethic.

The age of Dr Carlang variously appeared as 45 or 46 in the different publications and he was a divorcee with no children. He had been admitted to hospital with chest pains and had died of a heart attack in hospital a few days later. Parrish knew from experience that an obese man in his mid-forties might well be expected to die from a heart attack. As he had also died in hospital, foul play would be considered unlikely. Busy coroners and police forces were not required to investigate and would not waste any time with such a death.

Parrish initially tried to find more out about Dr Carlang through the Embleton University website. That search proved fruitless. The university had already removed all trace of him, other than the obituary. This told Parrish that it was likely that Dr Carlang was not held in high regard at the university, confirming implicitly what Parrish already suspected.

Universities, like many organisations, implement IT in many different ways and to similarly varied degrees of professionalism. There are many ways to uncover information that was meant to be hidden from view. During his career, DCI Parrish had learned about such techniques, although he had rarely undertaken such work himself. His detectives and other staff had done that for him. Now he would have to attempt the same himself.

It wasn't necessary to go beyond the simplest of ways to probe for information held by the university on Dr Carlang. Whoever had been responsible for maintaining the university website had been lazy.

They had merely deleted the links from the website to the web pages with information on Dr Carlang. The web pages on him still sat in cyberspace for anyone to view via a quick Google search with a few keywords.

The web pages confirmed what Parrish had suspected about Carlang. John Carlang had read Geography as an undergraduate at Embleton University and never left. He followed his Bachelor degree with a Masters degree and then a PhD to become Dr Carlang.

After gaining his PhD, Dr Carlang had been briefly employed as a Post-Doctoral Researcher before accepting a post as a Lecturer. His PhD and research career had resulted in five publications in peer-reviewed journals. Parrish could find no evidence of any research grants that Carlang had brought into Embleton. Despite being an academic at Embleton for about twenty years, Carlang had never become a Senior Lecturer. No mention was made of any positions he had held other than module leader.

Not quite the 'remarkable career' mentioned in his obituary. In fact, it was remarkable how little he had achieved in his career. The obituary had been written like a reference given to a former member of staff, which the former employer was rather glad so see the back of.

Parrish pondered over the '*dedicated academic*' reference in the obituary. *Was it written simply because Carlang had only ever been at Embleton University? Was it that he was actually a good lecturer and dedicated to his students? Could it be that he was subservient to the university, a yes-man?*

It was a fact that Carlang had only studied and worked at Embleton. Parrish searched Google, LinkedIn, Facebook and Instagram, but failed to pull up anything that suggested his students were fond of Carlang. Not a fact, but Parrish considered it unlikely that Carlang was a good lecturer who worked hard for his students.

Was Carlang a yes-man? This was very likely. Over a period of two decades, most large organisations will likely have at least a couple of reorganisations. Carlang had not been an active researcher after being appointed to Lecturer. This meant he had not published peer-reviewed articles or brought in grant money that were vital to not only promotion, but keeping an academic job at a university in a reshuffle.

So, Carlang had remained at Embleton by being subservient. But what had he done? He had to have done something useful to the university to have kept his job for so long. Parrish already had some questions for Robbie when they were to meet the following week.

Before then, he still had more detective work to do. At face value, the reports of the demise of Natasha

Horseman were more interesting to Parrish. She had apparently committed suicide. Her body had been found at the foot of some cliffs near Dunstanburgh Castle.

The various news reports and her obituary on the Embleton University website showed three different images of Natasha. In none of the pictures was she smiling.

Almost any picture of a drug dealer, vicious thug or killer, shown by the media, will likely portray them to be sullen, angry, or unpleasant in some way. By contrast, anyone who had been murdered or attacked by such people, will almost invariably show them smiling and happy.

When someone commits suicide, it is a trickier issue for a journalist when choosing an image. If possible, an image showing a neutral expression is best. Often, an image of the deceased isn't used, rather the location where it occurred or even simply the coroners court.

Three different pictures of Natasha. So, multiple pictures of her existed. All pictures of her were what Parrish thought of as neutral or sad. *Was that because she had committed suicide, was it her normal pose, or was she troubled by something?* he wondered.

The publications put her age at twenty-eight. He thought she was likely to be active on social media given both her age and the variety of images.

Trawling through her social media provided some clues to the life of Natasha. Sometimes the absence of posts and photos provides clues to a person's life too. The absence of wedding photos, babies and children suggested she had neither married nor had children.

There were lots of pictures of foreign holidays and a couple of brand-new budget-level cars. She appeared to live with her partner in a recently built, small property, which was furnished with a large widescreen TV, newly bought furniture and knickknacks.

Natasha stated on her social media accounts that she worked at Embleton University, but that was the extent of her disclosure about her work. Her obituary had said she worked in Human Resources. Brain fog was starting to kick in and Parrish attempted to make a mental rather than typed note to find more out about her work later, but his memory was unreliable.

Her partner, Gary, appeared to work for a delivery company. He drove a fifteen-year-old Audi that would have been expensive when new. The pictures online showed he was clearly proud of it and probably thought it still held cachet. What Parrish knew from previous investigations was that newer cars like this depreciated rapidly and you get a lot for your money once they are several years old. But what you were buying was a money pit. Insurance, tax and maintenance are expensive, as they drink fuel and eat tyres.

Gary's social media accounts indicated to Parrish that he was a bit of a lad. There were lots of pictures of him drinking with friends and partying. *Was there infidelity in this partnership?* Parrish wondered.

The new and newly furnished property, the cars, foreign holidays and regular social life, gave Parrish cause to dig elsewhere. Having uncovered potentially expensive lifestyles, *how did Natasha and Gary fund all this? Perhaps they were in debt?*

Once again, the Embleton University website proved porous. Natasha had joined the university straight from school on an apprenticeship. She had slowly made it into HR and held a lowly position there. The pay rates were available online and Parrish determined she earned about £27,400 per annum.

He next put this information into the HMRC tax calculator, which calculated that her monthly take home pay after tax would be approximately £1890. A quick look at car finance for the type of car she drove would be £250 per month. Rents in the area where she lived were about £850 per month.

Parrish stopped looking further. He could have looked into Gary's possible earnings but there were too many unknowns. It was unlikely that they were able to save much money and yet they may have been able to manage on their joint income.

It was equally possible that they might have large debts if they weren't careful with their spending. Simply armed with Google, social media and the internet, Parrish wasn't going to make much more concrete progress. Unlike his days in CID with resources available to look into the lives and finances of people in detail.

He had been working furiously for several hours. He already had questions about Dr Carlang. Now he had queries about the finances of Natasha and Gary. He also had questions about their relationship. *Was it rock steady or was Gary playing away from home?* Natasha might also be, but his intuition told him this was unlikely.

The bigger question was, did Natasha commit suicide? If she didn't, who murdered her? Who had motive and opportunity?

Chapter 4 – Pacing

From the coffee table, his phone chimed. It was the 2 pm daily alarm to remind him to take his second naproxen of the day. Parrish exhaled long and slowly, slightly miffed that his work had been interrupted.

He had loved these last few hours, a reminder of days gone by and the career he had loved and lost. Much like his wife. In the kitchen he took a naproxen from the blister pack and swallowed it down with a few glugs of cool water taken from the tap.

Staring out of the window as he stood at the kitchen sink, he realised how few resources he had and how many unknowns he had in this possible case. Meeting Robbie next week would be exciting, learning about the 'coincidences' that Robbie had mentioned.

His stomach grumbled. Engrossed with his work, Parrish had forgotten to eat and it was now two hours passed his usual meal time. *What to eat and what to do next?* He wondered. His chronic illnesses forced him to pace himself and plan his activities. If he did too much, he would pay for it dearly with a 'crash', confined to bed for days, weeks or even months.

He already knew that he had possibly done too much today with his mental activities researching the case. At least it was a Thursday, a day he reserved to do light to moderate activities. Thursdays were used to mow the lawn in the summer and cut up firewood in the winter, plus other more enjoyable activities such as riding his Honda 350 cc scooter.

As he was excited and felt he had done some good work, he decided to treat himself. Sliding his feet into his lined crocs, he put on his waxed jacket which bulged around his midriff and donned a flat cap to keep his bald head warm. Locking the front door of the old stone cottage behind him, he walked the short distance to the market square in the centre of Helmsley with his now deliberate slow gait since becoming chronically ill. Walking at what would have previously been his normal pace would increase his heart rate and metabolism. That would burn up his precious energy, filling his muscles with lactic acid due to ME affecting his metabolism.

Ever since a teenager, Parrish had often worn dealer boots with elasticated sides. They had been extremely fashionable for five minutes in the early 1980's, popularised by a band whose band members all wore them. But dealer boots were a classic design and had stood the test of time. Parrish had appreciated the ease with which you could quickly squeeze your feet in and out with a helping hand and without the need to tie laces.

Now though, the pain in his joints meant bending down to put boots on, was something only for special occasions. Parrish mainly wore slip-on sandals, slippers or one of his three pairs of crocs. The pair he wore during the warmer months were the classic croc with holes in the upper. During the colder months he wore the crocs he had on now. These sufficed in light rain too, but he had a third pair with no holes in the upper for particularly inclement weather.

Having arrived at the market square, he bought a steak pie from the butchers on the corner. If he hadn't had a coffee earlier, he might have had one now. He decided to sit on the steps of the Lord Feversham monument in the centre of the square to watch and listen to the bikers.

Archaeologists believe that the site of Helmsley was colonised from as early as 3000 BC. Helmsley certainly existed by 1086 because it is recorded in The Domesday Book, completed at the behest of William the Conqueror. It is a beautiful market town nestled at the base of the North Yorkshire Moors before the flat of the Vale of Pickering and York.

It's also a popular place for bikers and the local council had provided a large parking area dedicated for motorcycles. For years, the many businesses in this small market town had benefitted from the thousands of bikers who visited during the warmer and drier months. The council later decided in their infinite wisdom to charge for parking motorcycles there, which deterred many bikers and hurt local businesses.

Around the market square and down the narrow streets running off it, the bikers who still visited could buy fish and chips, ice creams, sandwiches, pies and drinks. Then they could sit on the benches around the square to eat and chat, or sit on the steps of the monument as Parrish was doing now.

He had deliberately chosen his outfit today, looking more like a local than a biker. If he didn't engage anyone in conversation, he could sit almost invisible to the bikers as they chatted together about their rides and their adventures. With a wry smile and occasional shake of the head, Parrish enjoyed listening to the exaggerated nonsense some of the biking fraternity came out with.

With his pie long since finished and bored listening to some Triumph enthusiasts talking in detail about the differences between the various models of Bonneville, Parrish headed for The Feathers across the road. Once inside, Parrish couldn't remember the staff. A pretty blonde waitress of about thirty years old, smiled at him knowingly in recognition from behind the bar.

'The usual Mr P?' she asked.

'Yes please,' he answered, recognising he was engulfed in brain fog. She clearly knew him and his favourite drink, yet he couldn't recall her, let alone her name. He sat down and as he slowly drank his wine, attempting to recollect the staff in the pub. Absolutely nothing was coming back to him, so he finished his drink then headed for home. Once home, Parrish went straight to bed and laid in the quiet and dark to begin recharging his batteries, trying to avoid a crash.

Chapter 5 – An old trick

The following Tuesday evening, Parrish sat waiting expectantly on his Chesterfield recliner in his living room. Robbie was due about six, half six, Parrish estimated. He had Googled the conference Robbie was attending in Tadcaster. The meeting broke for tea or coffee at 4:30 pm. Parrish reasoned that Robbie would likely mingle with his peers until about 5 pm. It wasn't a long drive by distance from Tadcaster to Helmsley, but the roads were tight and twisty, plus York commuter traffic at that time would slow Robbie.

The need Parrish felt to know every little detail about things had served him well as a detective. Unfortunately, it didn't serve him quite so well with friendships and relationships. His interest in minor details had often come across as intrusive or just plain weird to others.

A knock at the door signalled Robbie's arrival. Upon opening the door for his friend, Parrish could see Robbie beaming, as he was himself. It had been too long since these good friends had met and they shook hands firmly.

'Come in, come in,' welcomed Parrish.

'Good to see you, Scratcher, it's been too long.'

'Can I take your bags?'

'No, that's OK. If you don't mind, tell me where I am sleeping and I'll freshen up.'

'Up the stairs, second door on the left is your room. Bathroom and toilet are at the end of the corridor. If you find yourself in a cupboard, you've got the wrong door,' laughed Parrish.

A few minutes later and Parrish could hear the creaky stairs as Robbie descended to the living room. Robbie was dressed as sharp as ever, a habitually well-tailored chap. Creatures of habit; they had a brief conversation before heading out for something to eat.

Both men enjoyed good food and fine wine, so Parrish had booked them a table at the Feversham Arms. Not only would they enjoy tasty food and beverages with good service, but it would likely be quiet on a Tuesday evening. This would allow them to discuss matters without being overheard.

Over the meal, the two men caught up on events in the hiatus since their last meeting. Once the food was finished and a bottle of merlot opened, they finally got to the reason for their catch up. Robbie first asked if Parrish had read up on the deaths of Dr Carlang and Natasha Horseman. A nod of the head confirmed that he had.

'Did you find anything unusual about the deaths?' asked Robbie, 'I don't believe in coincidences but how this all fits together escapes me.'

'With only what I could find on the internet and without the resources I used to have at my disposal, I had a lot of blanks to fill in.'

'Do tell,' asked an eager Robbie.

'Reading between the lines and with quite a lot of presumption, I'd say Dr Carlang was a yes-man, eager to do the bidding of the university.'

'How did you arrive at that?'

'He had been at the university for two decades and survived probable reorganisations without being an active researcher or career academic.'

'Very good. You've lost none of your insight...And Natasha?'

'She'd been at the university since leaving school. She hadn't progressed spectacularly but had a safe, steady job. I've looked into her lifestyle, partner, holidays, cars, etc. and done a few calculations. Without more reliable information, I can't comment further.'

'Impressive stuff, Scratcher, but you haven't said anything about their deaths.'

Parrish explained that both deaths were entirely plausible. Without further information, it was impossible to draw either conclusions or progress his 'curiosities'. He had deliberately used the word 'curiosities' as opposed to 'investigations', which had drawn a smile from Robbie who instinctively recognised the use of language by Parrish.

'You never surprise me with your insight, Scratcher. My path had only crossed with Dr Carlang in various meetings. Always seemed lazy and a bit wet to me. I had a little more to do with Natasha as she dealt with mundane HR matters for me and my staff. Nothing remarkable though, until about a year ago.'

Robbie explained that Natasha had brought complaints to him about two of his staff, Dr Elfyn Williams and Dr Bear Lawrence. Both were talented lecturers who supported Robbie on a first-year module, 'Design and Mechatronics', which he was module leader for. The complaints were trivial at best and unworthy of anything other than a conversation between himself and Natasha. However, Natasha had insisted on holding formal meetings with herself, Robbie and either Elfyn or Bear.

Both men had reacted at their meeting as Robbie had expected. They had explained their actions and questioned the need for the meeting. Clearly, both men felt aggrieved at the alleged complaints. At the time, Robbie explained that he thought raising these 'complaints' in the manner Natasha had, was a little unusual. With hindsight, he recognised they were part of a pattern of behaviour of upper management towards these two members of staff.

Robbie explained that after three years of work at Embleton University, academics were entitled to a sabbatical for one semester. During a sabbatical, staff were not allowed to perform any of their normal duties. They were given complete freedom to undertake research, write academic papers, books and the like. They could also visit other relevant institutions or companies to improve their knowledge and contacts for the benefit of the university and their work.

It had been over thirteen years since Robbie had joined Embleton University. Despite being entitled to take a sabbatical, he had been putting it off for a decade. He was already an active researcher and prolific writer. A sabbatical would likely cause him more difficulties than benefits. Now the upper management were insistent that he took one at the start of the academic year, which was not long after the complaints against his colleagues.

Whilst away from the university, the Head of the School of Engineering had phoned him one day. Napoleon, as the Head had been nicknamed by his staff for his short stature and bullying nature, informed Robbie that both Elfyn and Bear had been suspended earlier that day.

Shocked, Robbie had asked why. He had been told only that it was for 'sexist remarks and mistreatment of students on Design and Mechatronics'. Napoleon refused to expand on this explanation and demanded that Robbie have no further contact with his two colleagues until further notice and that the entire matter was strictly confidential.

'Wow!', exclaimed Parrish, 'Sounds like a fit up. Did you have cause to believe such accusations?'

'Not in the slightest. These were colleagues I respected professionally for both their engineering and teaching abilities. I was module leader of Design and Mechatronics and had championed the cause of female students. It is incredulous to believe that I would have accepted any such behaviour.'

'What happened next? Did you speak to Elfyn or Bear?'

Robbie explained that he had briefly spoken to both men later that same day. Neither had a clue what the allegations might be and both were extremely distressed. He then had no further communications with them for some time.

The first contact with Bear was about four months later. Bear had asked Robbie via HR to attend a meeting with him at the university to discuss the complaints. When Robbie read the allegations, which were allegations against either Bear and Elfyn but now combined together to add weight against both

41

men, he was utterly stunned. He could neither believe they were true, nor that they merited suspension by the university.

'How did the meeting go?' asked Parrish.

'Immediately before the meeting, I met Bear. I was staggered by his health and appearance. It was clear this whole thing was taking a terrible toll on his mental and physical health. The meeting lasted an hour and involved Dr Carlang, who was the Complaints Manager, a woman from HR called Charlee Butcher, and a note taker.

'Bear was questioned and needless to say, the questions weren't for the benefit of Bear to exonerate himself. When we got the minutes of the meeting from Charlee Butcher, anything Bear had said that helped his case was omitted. When we challenged the notes, only a few changes were accepted that were of little consequence. For those things that did matter, the reply from Charlee Butcher was that the university records from her and the note taker didn't match what we claimed.'

'A complete fit up. What happened next?'

'Bear asked me to attend a grievance meeting, a complaint of his against the university. We met another woman from HR and the Grievance Manager, no note taker was provided this time. The Grievance Manager obviously hadn't read the grievance, didn't know the rules and didn't care one jot. That was until towards the end of the meeting.'

'Sounds intriguing?'

'Bear asked if his grievance was confidential, which they confirmed. He asked similarly, would the staff dealing with the complaints know anything about his grievance, which they confirmed would not be the case. Then he dropped a bombshell. He proved that Charlee Butcher had accessed his grievance. She had lifted a section of his written grievance word-for-word and put it in the minutes from the complaint meeting.'

'Really?'

'Like us, Bear can smell a rat. He set Butcher up by reading a pre-written statement at the complaint meeting. It sounded exactly like part of his written grievance. Crucially, it wasn't, she had swapped the order of a couple of sentences and changed a few words. Butcher must have read the grievance beforehand and recognised what he read out. She lifted the words from the grievance and put them in the minutes of the meeting. Then she accepted our changes to the minutes to correct them to what he had read out, versus what he had written in the grievance.'

'What were the consequences of that?'

'I didn't find out until months later. She was found guilty of a breach of confidentiality, but it was considered immaterial that she knew the details of the grievance. It was just brushed under the mat.'

Parrish sat back in his chair and took a sip of wine whilst he considered what he had listened to. 'You've mentioned Dr Carlang was the Complaints Manager and Natasha was involved in some trivial complaints against your two colleagues. These colleagues were suspended, whilst you were forced away from the university on sabbatical. Let me take a wild stab in the dark, neither of these colleagues are still at the university.'

'Bingo. I received an email out of the blue from Charlee Butcher. It said I was to now deal with both these men under the Absence and Sickness Policy as their Line Manager. I explained that Napoleon had forbidden me to speak to either of them and questioned her on a few things. She ignored everything I asked and insisted I treat them under the Absence and Sickness policy. What I suspected was confirmed, the university had been actively trying to subject them to the Disciplinary Process. Elfyn submitted his resignation, which was accepted. Bear had a nervous breakdown and they held a Disciplinary Meeting in his absence and dismissed him.'

Parrish picked up the bottle of merlot and recharged both glasses. They sat in silence for a minute for

Parrish to process the information. 'It's shocking how a university can treat staff. Like you, I don't believe in coincidences. However, at the moment it's a big jump to murder for two deaths that the police didn't consider suspicious. The basis of which is HR are suspected of fitting up two members of staff in order to remove them from the university.'

'I quite agree. But there is a third incident that I have not mentioned.'

'Why not, I could have looked into it before today?'

'You couldn't have looked it up, that's why. The university have done their best to eliminate all traces of it. One of the students who made allegations against Elfyn and Bear, later made another allegation. She claimed to have been sexually assaulted by Mr Bruce Wells, in his office. Bruce is the fourth member of academic staff to support Design and Mechatronics; Elfyn, Bear, Bruce and myself.'

Parrish was visibly shocked, his mouth open.

'Given the severity of the accusation, the university was obliged to bring in the police. Bruce was suspended like the other two colleagues and I was again told not to talk to him or anyone else about the matter.'

'What happened?'

'The police investigated and it soon became apparent that she had fabricated the allegations. She provided a date and time, which Bruce had an alibi for. So, she provided another date and time, which Bruce also had an alibi for. Rumour has it, she was also unable to describe his office, other than what she could see from the door window. She had obviously never been inside.'

'Is Bruce still at the university?'

'They reinstated him but changed his role. His only contact with students is either via zoom or when giving lectures, which are recorded. The sudden disappearance of Elfyn and Bear caused some discontent amongst staff and students. I suspect it was the student disquiet that prevented the immediate departure of Bruce, plus the fact he was exonerated by the police investigation.'

'What happened to the student?'

'It's all rumour mill, but she was apparently given an official warning by the police for wasting their time. As for the university, she's still there paying her fees, which is all the university hierarchy are really interested in.'

'That all sheds a different light on what you have told me. You are effectively forced out of the university by senior management making you take a sabbatical. They could have done that at any time in the previous decade so the timing is suspicious. Two of your colleagues on the same module are then effectively dismissed. Next, allegations are made against a third colleague. That only leaves one other member of academic staff on that module, you. You need to watch your back Robbie; the knives are out for you.'

'That may be true. But without blowing my own trumpet I'm a senior professor, the university would be less inclined to have a go at me. Especially, when you consider that Bruce is still here and escaped the full wrath of senior management, for now at least.'

'I wasn't just referring to the university. Elfyn and Bear both had cause to feel disgruntled with both Carlang and Horseman, not to mention Charlee Butcher. The students who made the complaints, however insignificant and unlikely you may consider the complaints to be, may still hold a grudge against both men. One of them seemingly had it in for Bruce too, which may mean that you are on her radar.'

Once again, they sat in silence; Parrish processing what he had just been told and Robbie hoping expectedly that his old friend might find some insight and inspiration.

Parrish leant forward and picked up the bottle of merlot, which he found to be empty. 'Another here or should we retire to the cottage for more wine or some port?'

'Port sounds good to me.'

'Great, I'll try and catch the waiter.'

'No need my old friend, it's all sorted.'

'Well thank you, but you shouldn't have. You paid when I went to the bathroom earlier?'

'Yes, that old trick.'

Chapter 6 – Golf

When Parrish eventually descended the stairs of the cottage the following morning, Robbie had left him a note. It thanked Parrish for his hospitality and hoped that they would be in touch again soon.

Wednesday would normally have been a rest day for Parrish, which was fortunate. Meeting his friend the previous evening had been enjoyable but energy sapping. Whilst Parrish would now rest physically, he knew he would be using both mental energy thinking about what he had learned and emotional energy worrying about his friend. He knew he may crash as a result.

So, Parrish returned to bed. Towards the end of the week, he could have possibly got up and completed a few chores. But he knew better than to do that from experience and elected to relocate to the living room watching TV whilst he managed his energy levels.

By Monday, Parrish had decided to ring a former colleague. DCI Andy Thompson had been stationed in Embleton and was part of the Northumberland and Cheviots Police Force. Their paths had crossed several times over the years, not least with the infamous case of Raoul Moat.

Andy Thompson was older than Parrish and now also retired. It was likely that Andy would know the detective who had replaced him at the Northumberland and Cheviots Police CID. Parrish had decided to call Andy first to discuss the 'case', rather than whoever the current incumbent was.

Since Robbie had asked Parrish to look into Dr Carlang and Natasha Horseman, Parrish had been excited to have a new case to work on. In the days that followed the meeting, Parrish had come to the same conclusion as Robbie that there were simply too many coincidences. However, there was probably too little to go on for an over-worked police force to be interested.

Parrish rang Andy, but it went straight to voicemail. A few hours later, Andy rang back and apologised for missing the call, he had been on the golf course. A long conversation followed in which Parrish presented the information in a very different manner to which he had learned it.

He had begun the story very much like the presentations he gave at conferences for detectives, coroners and the like. His mantra for presentations was the same as many others, 'tell them what you are going to tell them, tell them, tell them what you told them.'

Parrish told Andy of the suspicions of foul play held by Robbie based on too many coincidences. A description of the Design and Mechatronics course and staff set the stage. Then the timeline of events then followed: the raising of minor complaints, Robbie's forced sabbatical, the suspension and ultimate university departure of Dr's Williams and Lawrence, the unfounded allegation of a sexual assault, the untimely death of Dr Carlang and finally the apparent suicide of Natasha Horseman.

It was at this juncture that Parrish's narrative was interrupted by Andy asking questions. Not that it mattered, Andy asked pertinent questions about the various staff involved and more. This was all what Parrish had intended to say anyway.

Towards the end of the conversation, Andy promised to give it all some thought. He explained to Parrish that he was playing golf the following weekend with DCI Stephen Alexanderson, his replacement in CID. Over golf he would discuss matters with the current DCI, if he had decided they merited such. Parrish could hope for no more and they wished each other well.

Over a round of golf, Andy explained to DCI Alexanderson how he knew Parrish. DCI Stephen Alexanderson had of course heard of Parrish by reputation, as he had been a colossus in his professional world. That reputation, coupled with a healthy respect, had given Andy the confidence to voice his concerns about what were still fairly abstract events. Likewise, it was with the same reputation and respect for Parrish that DCI Alexanderson listened and questioned Andy over eighteen and particularly the nineteenth hole.

'As you know, I have the utmost respect for DCI Parrish', Stephen told Andy.

'If he was still a serving officer then I would have met with him to discuss it, if nothing more than to meet the great man. I would also have documented his concerns in case there was something in this and it came back to haunt me, had I neglected them.

'Unfortunately, we live in an age of budgets and staff cuts. My time is too precious to devote to what my superiors might consider a flight of fancy. Equally, I cannot ask my staff to look at the cases of Dr Carlang and Natasha Horseman. They are time and resource pressurised professionals and I must trust in their and the medical professional's judgement and findings. Having said that, if anything further comes to light, I would appreciate you or DCI Parrish letting me know immediately. I don't need to tell you that a good detective always has a nose for these things.'

It was the following day when Andy rang Parrish with news of the conversation over golf. Parrish had expected as much of the outcome, although the obvious respect for his reputation was humbling. As a bonus, he now had the number for DCI Alexanderson if anything new came up.

In another telephone conversation that evening, Parrish relayed the news to a disappointed but equally unsurprised Professor Robbie Mustoe.

Chapter 7 – Missing person

A couple of weeks later and Robbie rang Parrish one evening. 'I have some news, Scratcher.'

'About this case, if I can call it that, or are you finally going to make an honest woman of Christine?' chuckled Parrish.

Parrish could hear Robbie smiling when he replied, 'I attended a committee meeting at the university this morning. It was the usual boring affair, save for one interesting observation.'

'Oh, yes?'

'Charlee Butcher should have been there. She hardly ever misses one and always offers her apologies beforehand if she can't attend.'

'I take it she didn't email to explain she would be absent?'

'No, she didn't. I rang HR on the pretence of another matter and during the conversation I mentioned in passing that she missed the meeting. She was in on Monday, but hasn't been in since. Nobody at work has heard from her. It's not like her at all, apparently.'

'Do you know if she has been reported missing?'

'No, I thought that a bit much to bring into the conversation. It would certainly be a red flag if this turns out to be as serious as we think it may be.'

'If you don't mind Robbie, I'll ring DCI Alexanderson and tell him this.'

'Fine by me.'

Immediately after the call to Robbie, Parrish rang the DCI. After introductory pleasantries, Parrish said, 'it might be nothing but I hoped you might like to know something that has caught my interest.'

'Go on.'

'You may remember the name Charlee Butcher from the information Andy relayed to you. She was the linchpin in the removal of Dr Williams and Dr Lawrence from Embleton University. Charlee Butcher also worked with Dr Carlang and Natasha Horseman, both of whom are now deceased.'

'I expect she's not on the Christmas card lists for either Dr Williams or Dr Lawrence. What else have you got for me?'

'She's gone missing.'

'Let me check the missing persons database whilst we keep talking.'

'Charlee Butcher hasn't turned in for work since Monday at the university, and nobody there has heard a peep from her. I'm told that is highly unusual for her.'

'Nothing coming up on Charlee Butcher. What else do you know about her?'

'Only that she's utterly ruthless in destroying careers by the sound of it.'

'You understand that I can't act on this unless she is reported missing. Even if I could, I haven't the resources to look into a possible misper.'

'Of course, but this one smells. You did ask me to let you know if anything else came to light.'

'I do appreciate it, thank you.'

Chapter 8 – The first 24 hours

It was Friday morning and DCI Stephen Alexanderson was sat at his desk in HQ. His phone vibrated in his pocket and he took it out. DI Morter was calling. 'Mick, what is it?'

'Body, Sir, IC-one female. Dog walker found it in woods near Fallodon Hall. I'm here with DS Ash.'

'What else?'

'Blonde, curly, shoulder-length hair. Taller than average, maybe 5'8", athletic build. Looks like she may have been out running judging by her clothes, which have been partially removed. Looks to have been hit on the head. SOCO and the pathologist are on the way.'

'Any ID?'

'She's wearing a phone on her left upper arm. Difficult to see anything else as she's face down.'

'You know the drill, Mick, cordon off the area, get some boots on the ground and call in the dog squad. Let me know as soon as you have anything else. I'll arrange a staff meeting and media briefing for later.'

'Yes Sir.'

* * *

DCI Stephen Alexanderson called a meeting for every member of CID at noon. Those not present in HQ were expected to join the meeting via zoom. 'Thank you everyone. This will be short by necessity. As you know the first twenty-four hours are critical to getting a quick result. We've got an IC-one deceased female, partially dressed in purple athletic gear in the woods near Fallodon Hall. As is often the case, the body was found by a dog walker. Looks like she's been bludgeoned on the head. DI Morter is at the scene and will be the lead investigator on this one. You'll find a description of the deceased, location, etc. on the case database. DI Morter, what more can you tell us?'

The handsome chiselled face of DI Morter with his neat, short dark brown hair was already on a large screen in the office. 'The pathologist has confirmed the death but not the cause of it. The victim has been both bludgeoned and strangled. We won't know for sure until the post-mortem which was the cause of death.'

'OK. Any signs of a struggle or fight?'

'No. The pathologist doesn't think that this is the murder location and I agree with that. She could have been dumped there.'

'What about possible sexual assault or rape?'

'Her top was pulled up to expose her breasts and her shorts and knickers pulled down to her knees.

The pathologist said that he could see nothing obvious that might indicate a sexual assault, but he needs to do the post-mortem before he can make further comment.'

'Time of death?'

'Best guess for now is a few days ago, probably less than a week.'

'Have you secured the woods and the footpaths in the area?'

'We initially secured the immediate area, we're now extending that. The problem we have is that there are several paths, tracks and a lot of woodland around the deposit site. I've got DS Ash supervising uniform.'

'Good work, but not so good for finding evidence. Speak to me before the next briefing. I'd like maps with areas prioritised for searches. Do we know who she is yet?'

'She has a phone strapped to her upper arm, like you see runner's wear. SOCO says the phone is locked. They'll need to get it back to the labs to try and get into it. Other than that, nothing, no purse, ID or jewellery other than some stud earrings.'

'Can you prepare a statement to release to the media please?'

'Certainly Sir. I'll run it by you before it's released.'

DCI Alexanderson had been watching DI Morter on the big screen. He now turned to the room. 'DC Walker. I want you to contact Embleton University ASAP. Get through to HR, ask them about a Charlee Butcher, we want a physical description and photos plus some background info; what she does, where she lives, friends, next of kin, and so on. Until after the media briefing, make no mention of this body. Tell them you're following up a misper report if you have to.'

'We've not had a misper report for a Charlee Butcher, Sir,' said a surprised DS Walker, whose role included managing and investigating missing persons.

'I know that. Just call it a copper's nose.'

* * *

Within an hour, DC Walker had forwarded a description and two photos of Charlee Butcher from the university to DI Morter and the pathologist. They were in agreement that the deceased appeared to be Charlee Butcher. DI Morter then rang DCI Alexanderson who answered the phone almost immediately. 'Mick.'

'Looks like you were right Sir, we think it's Charlee Butcher.'

'What do you know about her next of kin?'

'Two elderly parents living on the Isle of Wight. Who will be Family Liaison on this one Sir?'

'From memory it will be DC's Nicola Butters and Stuart Wilkinson. It's not like in our day, one job after another as FLO. I'll have to double check my records to make sure it's been at least twelve months since they were active FLO's and that they've passed assessments to return to duty in that role.'

'They've got a long trip ahead of them, down there and back, plus two ferry journeys.'

'It's never an easy job being an FLO, as we both know.'

Chapter 9 – Hours 24 to 48

First thing the following morning, DCI Alexanderson held another CID meeting. It was a Saturday, but nobody was voicing complaint at having to be in work. They were 24 hours into the murder investigation. 'Good morning, everybody. Thanks for your efforts late into yesterday. I'll let DI Morter take it from here.'

DI Morter was sat alongside him in the largest investigation room in HQ. 'Thank you, Sir. I'll summarise what we know so far. As usual everyone, stop me if you have more information or to update us all on your progress.

'We have a confident, but unconfirmed, ID on the victim. We think she is Charlee Butcher, 38 years old, worked in HR at Embleton University. The postmortem took place late yesterday. We know that she's 5'9", slim athletic build, blonde curly shoulder length hair. She has blunt trauma to the upper rear skull, which likely knocked her unconscious. Death was by asphyxiation with a thin ligature, which we have yet to find. There were some microscopic fibres, a polymer of some sort, of various colours where the ligature was applied. Our first thoughts are that the killer has used climbing cord or rope, possibly a thin belt.

'There were no signs of sexual assault or rape, despite the partially undressed state of the body. Various tests are still coming through but it looks like she was sober, no drugs in her system, no other complications or factors other than the head trauma and strangulation. Similarly, we have very little information about the killer at this time. It appears that they were forensically aware. DC Walker, any more on the victim?'

'Apparently, she was quite private. Her boss could only tell me that she's likely single and lives alone, was dedicated to work and an exercise fanatic. Next of kin are her parents who are travelling up from the Isle of Wight with the FLO's, DC's Nicola Butters and Stuart Wilkinson. Hopefully, we'll get the ID completed early this afternoon sometime.'

'Thank you.' DI Morter turned back to the room and continued. 'The location where her body was found, was probably not where she was struck on the head. DS Ash was on the scene until late yesterday. She has uploaded images and maps of the scene to the server. One of these is a prioritised search map because we have a large search area to cover and the searches are continuing under her supervision. We expect that there could be all manner of items in and around the woods. To more efficiently search the area, we are interested in anything that looks like it's been there less than a week. Anything to add, DS Ash?'

'A second area of interest has now been identified. It's a style over a fence that crosses a footpath. The footpath runs near to where the body was found. The search team think there is blood on the ground and what appear to be heavy footprints in the mud. The area has been secured and SOCO are on their way there.'

'Thank you, DS Ash. DC Smith, any more on the phone that was recovered?'

'Yes, Sir, but it's not what we might have hoped for. It's a two-year old smart phone, nothing on it, looks like it's had a factory reset. Curiously, it didn't have a SIM card or an electronic SIM. I've requested the phone records of the deceased from the phone number provided by her boss and confirmed by her parents, plus a trace of where it's been from the telecommunication mast pings.'

'Thank you, DC Smith.' DI Morter continued, 'We need to confirm the ID of the victim ASAP. DS Ash, we need eye-witnesses and interviews, plus check all those on the sex offenders list who live locally, they need confirmed alibis.'

'Yes Sir. Not a lot of doors to knock on but we'll ask at Fallodon Hall, nearby farms and cottages. We've had a surge in rural crime in the last few months so we might be able to collect CCTV too, which many landowners have now fitted.'

DI Morter turned to look at another colleague. 'DC Smith, can you see if any of our cars were in the vicinity in the last few days and pull any ANPR data. We might hit lucky with a number plate from a possible suspect as the investigation develops. Also, get the ball rolling on other potential digital evidence; bank accounts, credit cards, emails, social media, online auction sites, etc.'

'Yes Sir.'

'DC Walker. Make arrangements and a schedule to interview any family and friends, her immediate boss and colleagues. Contact the local gyms. Likelihood is she's a regular somewhere. DC Smith will pass on other witnesses that he might identify from the digital footprint. We want to check her house, car, place of work and anything else that comes up.'

DC Walker nodded and replied, 'Yes Sir.'

'That's all for now. Remember, we keep moving at pace at least until we hit 72 hours. Thank you everybody, keep me updated.'

DI Morter and the rest of the room turned to DCI Alexanderson, who was a huge man, 6'5" tall and broad-framed with it. He had a huge persona and was quietly spoken, his voice contrasting with both his huge size and reputation. He carried a gravitas, which commanded respect, as did his reputation for his abilities and his respect and trust of his fellow officers. 'DI Morter and DS Ash, keep up the good work with what is a difficult and very sizeable task. You have my backing on your decisions. My appreciation to all of you for your efforts so far. Let's keep it up so that we might get a quick result, thank you. DC Walker, would you come to my office please with DI Morter and DS Ash?'

Back in his office, DCI Alexanderson told them what he had learnt about the recent comings and goings within Embleton University. What DCI Alexanderson did not disclose was how he knew all this from DCI Parrish and they were smart enough not to ask.

* * *

Johnny Cash played on his phone, which disturbed Parrish who was watching a documentary about a conspiracy theory. The phone screen indicated it was DCI Alexanderson ringing him. 'DCI Alexanderson, great to hear from you?' said a happy Parrish.

Not one to beat about the bush, the DCI replied 'Likewise. Thought you'd like to know that we've found a body.'

He went on to explain the basics only; how a dog walker had found a body in rural Northumberland a couple of miles from Embleton. They suspected that it was Charlee Butcher, but she was still to be formerly identified.

'Thanks for sharing that information with me. Good luck, I hope you catch the killer very soon.'

'So do I.'

Chapter 10 – 48 to 72 hours

It was Sunday morning and they were 48 hours into the investigation. DI Morter was chairing the latest meeting at Police HQ. 'Thank you everyone for giving up your weekend and putting in the graft at such a crucial time.

'Charlee Butcher has been positively identified by her parents. Unfortunately, the parents haven't been close to her in recent years. They weren't able to give us much about her life. They believe she is single and lives alone, also lives for her work in HR at Embleton University and keeps fit in her own time. They think she may have kept in touch with a couple of university friends from when she did her undergraduate degree. They could only offer first names, Vicky and Elaine. DC Walker, what progress have you made on interviews?'

'Her boss, Heledd Morgan, is coming in at 11 am today. She's the Director of Human Resources at Embleton University.'

'Thank you. Everyone, I know it is Sunday, but do your best to rattle cages and get all the information we need as soon as possible, especially on the convicted sex offenders. Tomorrow, a forensic psychologist will be available to look at the case. For now, I believe the killer was male. He had the physical strength to knock her unconscious, carry her into the woods and then strangle her, plus there is the possible sexual angle. We can also assume that the murder was premeditated. The killer probably took a ligature with him and certainly took it away. He must have worn gloves too. We have recovered no fingerprints or DNA so far.

'He took her phone from the holder on her arm, completed a factory reset, removed the SIM card and replaced the phone in the holder. All that takes time, so he's a cool customer. I do wonder though, why he would do a reset and take the SIM? Why not simply take the phone with him and destroy it?'

'Perhaps he was worried about leaving a digital trace if signals pinged off the phone masts?' asked DC Smith.

'There is that to consider but this man would probably have known that. He could have turned it off and took it away with him. So why didn't he do that? Why did he do a factory reset and take the SIM? Was there something on there he was looking for before he wiped the phone? Was there something he thought was on there and wiped it? Did he use the phone to access cloud storage? Lots to consider on this. DC Smith, make this and Butcher's phone accounts your number one priority please.'

'You got it, Sir.'

* * *

DC Walker led Heledd Morgan to interview room one and she sat down on the chair suggested to her by DC Walker. Dressed in a plain, but expensive looking light green dress with matching thin belt, her long wavy ginger hair was held back with a large clasp and she wore both understated jewellery and makeup. All these she had carefully and deliberately chosen to appear welcoming, innocent, thoughtful and professional.

'Would you like a tea or coffee?' asked DC Walker.

'Water would be fine,' she replied in her soft Welsh accent.

He nodded and left the room to both fetch the water and to text DI Morter where she was waiting.

A few minutes later, DC Walker and DI Morter sat across the table from her. Both of them were smartly dressed too, attempting to look professional, relaxed and non-threatening. They both sported oversized shiny shackles on their left wrists. The brands, Longines and Omega, suitably aligned with their ranks of DS and DI respectively.

A well-practised routine began with DC Walker explaining that she had been invited to help them with the investigation into the murder of Charlee Butcher. At any time, she was free to go or have a solicitor with her. They were recording the interview from CCTV and a copy would be made available to her if she requested such.

DI Morter began the questioning. 'My condolences at the loss of your colleague.'

'Thank you.'

'And thank you for coming here on a Sunday to help with our enquiries.'

'It's the least I could do.'

'I would like to ask you some questions about Charlee Butcher. I appreciate that these may be a little upsetting for you, so just take your time and we can take a break at any point.'

She nodded coyly.

'Please would you tell me what Charlee was like as a person.'

'More than anything else, she was utterly professional. She had little time for chat. Most of her colleagues probably knew little about her as she generally worked alone in her office.'

This already spoke volumes to DI Morter. He knew that she was instrumental in the removal of Dr Elfyn Williams and Dr Bear Lawrence from the university. Given the manner that this had apparently been done, there would have been a need to keep things as confidential as possible. 'With you being her boss, perhaps she divulged a little about her personal life to you?'

'Yes, but surprisingly little. We are, were, both dedicated to our work. Both single, never married, no children. Health and fitness were the next biggest things for her. Always running and going to the gym. I got the impression she occasionally had a boyfriend, but she was very private about such matters.'

'Has she been any different lately, anything at all that you noticed?'

'Everyone in HR has been a little different recently.'

'Why so?'

'We lost a colleague, Natasha Horseman. She committed suicide at the cliffs near Dunstanburgh Castle recently.'

DI Morter knew this already, but he pretended otherwise. 'I am sorry. I had heard that but hadn't realised she worked in HR with you. Can you think of any other reason Charlee may not have been her usual self?'

'Not that I know of.'

'Thank you. It will be necessary to search her office and any computers, phones, etc. that she used. Warrants are being prepared for these.'

'I understand and the university will give you its full cooperation. I would ask that we liaise about these searches though. I have the reputation of the university to consider. It might not look so good to have a heavy police presence.'

DI Morter replied tersely. 'And I understand too. You must remember that this is a murder enquiry and we are doing our best to apprehend the person who killed your late colleague.'

DI Morter was trying to walk a fine line. He wanted the cooperation of the university and Heledd Morgan, but she needed to realise that he held the cards here. 'Please would you tell me a little about your role at the university?'

'Yes, of course. I am Director of Human Resources at Embleton University, which is the third largest employer in Northumberland with about six-thousand employees.'

'I had no idea how big your organisation was,' lied DI Morter, he had done his homework already.

'Few people do.'

'Can you perhaps explain how HR is organised and how you fit in to it?'

'Certainly. I'm at the top of the HR organisation, which at any given time has about forty members of staff. Below me in the organisation are business managers who report directly to me. The remaining staff report to them. The university has three faculties; Engineering and Science, Art and

Humanities, Accountancy and Business. Each faculty is supported by about ten to a dozen members of the HR team.'

DI Morter immediately recognised the lack of clarity in her answer, the numbers of staff she was presenting simply didn't add up. He decided to come back to that later and pressed on with his questioning. 'What is it that the HR team do please?

'In the main, much of it is fairly mundane and relates to the working lifetime of an employee.'

'I'm not sure that I follow you by the term 'working lifetime'.'

'In the beginning, the university will want to recruit for a position. We assist with the job description, advert and the recruiting process. Once a candidate is chosen, we then integrate them into the university systems, ensure they have the correct training, salary and pension, staff ID and other arrangements are all completed. Then for much of their time at the university there will be little to do. Occasionally, there may be promotions and pay rises to deal with, maternity leave, sick leave, and the like. Eventually, they will submit their notice or retire and we will ensure that any passes, keys, etc. are returned, that the pay arrangements are brought to a conclusion together with any necessary paperwork, such as a P45.'

Now, DI Morter allowed a silence to linger slightly longer than was necessary in a normal conversation. It was a deliberate tactic to unsettle the interviewee. 'There must be other things to deal with. Complaints about individuals for instance.'

'Yes of course. These matters are dealt with by our HR faculty teams.'

'Does that include very serious problems?'

'Our staff are very experienced. As the severity of the issues increases, more experienced and senior staff deal with them.'

Once again, DI Morter paused. What he knew of what happened to Bear Lawrence and Elfyn Williams, handled by Charlee Butcher, made him suspect that she might possibly have a special role within HR. His questions were slowly leading towards discovering what she did. 'Forgive me, but 'business manager' seems an odd job description for someone working in HR.'

'I took over this department just over two years ago. It was called the Personnel Department then and was notably failing. The previous director was removed from position and I was brought in to turn things around.'

'That's interesting and impressive. What changes did you make?'

'The first thing was to change the name of the department and the job roles. The Personnel Department became Human Resources and the faculty personnel managers became business managers'

'Was that sufficient to turn things around?'

'Not on their own. These were symptomatic of a change in attitude needed throughout all the HR staff. Embleton University is no different from any other university, which are all charities, technically. But they operate like large businesses. To maintain our size and reputation we must generate income, be efficient, promote the correct image and have good output, product, you might say. The HR staff and university upper management needed a new mind-set and I have been instrumental in changing that.'

'So, going back a step in my questions. The role of a business manager is to take care of business?'

'You might say that, yes.'

'Are the most serious issues dealt with by the business managers?'

'Yes, that would be the case.'

Things were building nicely as DI Morter saw it. He decided it was time to return to the issue of staff numbers. 'Please forgive me, maths isn't my strong point. If you have three faculties, each supported by ten or a dozen people from HR, you must have a few people assigned to different roles, such as yourself, to make up the full complement of forty people that you just mentioned?'

'Yes, those would be myself and the business managers.'

DI Morter sat thoughtfully for a few seconds before asking his next question. His maths was not weak. Three faculties of ten to a dozen staff came to between thirty and thirty-six staff. If each faculty was supported by one business manager, plus the director, that would come to thirty-four to forty members of staff. This meant that whilst her answer of 'forty members of staff' could be explained by her answer, it more likely meant that there were other persons unaccounted for. What he knew was that Charlee Butcher had been instrumental in the determined removal of two members of staff from the university. That may mean that she had a special role in this new, ruthless, business-orientated HR department. 'Are there any other members of HR staff who report directly to you?'

'No.'

'How many business managers are there?'

'Three.'

'One for each faculty?'

'Yes.'

DI Morter again took a little time to consider these replies. They weren't what he was expecting. 'Where did Charlee Butcher fit into your organisation and what was her role and responsibilities?'

'She was a business manager and like I have said, she reported directly to me.'

True answers, but deceitful at the same time, thought DI Morter. She had failed to say what Charlee Butcher actually did. 'So, Charlee Butcher was one of your three business managers?' asked DI Morter quizzically.

'She was one of four.'

'But you just said you have three business managers.'

'I did. Charlee Butcher is no longer a business manager.'

'Miss Morgan, you are expected to cooperate fully with an investigation. Impeding an investigation is a criminal offence.'

'And I am not under arrest and free to walk out of here at any time.'

'You are indeed. And I am able to get both a search warrant and arrest you tomorrow at the university in full view of both staff and students.'

They sat in silence after the heated exchange. DI Morter was purposely letting Heledd Morgan take time to fully appreciate what he was saying. 'I will repeat my earlier question. Where did Charlee Butcher fit into your organisation and what was her role and responsibilities?'

'She was a business manager and as you put it, responsible for taking care of business.'

'You have three faculties and had four business managers. Can I presume there were three managers for the three faculties and a fourth for other business?'

'Yes.' Heledd Morgan angrily replied.

'And the fourth business manager was presumably Charlee Butcher?'

'Yes.' She replied indignantly.

DI Morter paused again. He was ready to deliver a question that he thought might unsettle the Director. As he prepared to deliver it, he studied her body language and facial expression. Now he looked her in the eye and asked, 'Did she take care of business in the case of Dr Elfyn Williams and Dr Bear Lawrence?'

Her mouth opened and she sat upright in her chair. She was clearly shocked by the question. DI Morter took it all in and simply waited, leaving an uncomfortable silence for her to break. 'How did you know about those men?'

'I ask the questions in here.'

'Yes, she did,' retorted the director.

'Pretty rough treatment was doled out to those men, as I understand it.'

'I can assure you that we followed our written procedures.'

'Perhaps you did, but was it done 'reasonably'?'

Heledd Morgan scowled at him. 'Reasonably' was an employment law legal term. Employers were expected to behave reasonably and they seemingly had not acted reasonably in the case of Bear Lawrence and Elfyn Williams.

'If we are going to continue along these lines of enquiry then I want a solicitor present.'

'No need Director. I want a list of the people Charlee Butcher took care of business with since you took over HR by 10 am tomorrow morning. I want descriptions of what happened in each case and all the people involved. You have my assurances that this information will remain confidential. Thank you for your time today. In due course, I am sure we will be chatting again.'

With that the interview was over. Within three hours, DI Morter received a list of new suspects with possible motive to kill Charlee Butcher.

Chapter 11 – Outside the window

It was Monday morning and DI Morter stood before a crowded briefing room in CID. It was 72 hours since the body had been discovered. 'Good morning, everybody. Thank you for your efforts over the weekend. As you all know, the window of opportunity has gone to catch the killer quickly. That is not the only problem we have in solving this case.

'We know less about our victim, Charlee Butcher, than we would like to. She was a private person. Her colleagues are likely to know little about her. But they are all going to need interviewing.

'It seems she was a business manager in HR at Embleton University. She had a role in which she actively removed any staff or students who were considered to possibly harm the reputation of the university. And she was utterly ruthless in doing so. This means we have a long list of potential suspects to interview. Dr Bear Lawrence, Dr Elfyn Williams and eight students are our primary suspects at this stage.

'Another line of enquiry is Fountains Gym in Embleton. She went there regularly on evenings after work and on weekends. I want every gym member interviewing. Who did she chat to? Who knew this woman?

'Her neighbours have been interviewed already. None of them seem to know her beyond saying a passing hello. Her family live down south and see her infrequently. As soon as you can, put any new information you get into the database. There has to be a link somewhere to the killer through her work, neighbours, friends, the gym and so on.

'We've searched her property and have her car. These and various items are being examined including a work laptop we recovered. They could all hold vital clues. Also, we must find her phone. DS Ash is leading the search for that. We now know that it was taken from the holder on her arm and replaced by a burner phone of the same type. The killer took the phone and it was still switched on for a short time after her death because it pinged another mast so it was moved from the murder site towards Embleton. Unfortunately, there are few masts in that part of rural Northumberland and we can't get an accurate location for it.

'There will be a more detailed media release after this meeting. We've held it back deliberately. There were some big national news stories this weekend and the local news was full of Newcastle United playing Liverpool FC. We didn't want this story to get lost amongst other news.

'If you haven't already logged into the database, you'll soon see I've allocated duties to you all. Thank you and as usual keep me informed of any pertinent developments.'

* * *

Dr Justin Redpath was a tall man who dressed elegantly. He sat in CID across the desk from DI Morter. He was an arrogant man and delivered his forensic psychology reports as if they were 100 % accurate and never to be questioned. DI Morter loathed him but wanted every bit of help with his investigation that he could get. That included questioning the pompous psychologist on his report if he had to.

'The killer knew the victim and her routines. He knew she would be running along that footpath. She knew him so he was able to catch her off-guard when he struck her with the rock.

'He's tall and muscular. He carried her to the murder site. He chose both locations, so he is familiar with the area and did some reconnaissance. He's local, he's careful and a planner.

'He already had the rock to hand, it wasn't a random act. Similarly, the ligature he used he had with him and was careful to take it away. He wore gloves too, he knows about forensics.

'We know that it was premediated murder, by these facts and especially so having a burner phone and swapping it for her phone. He must know her extremely well. He swapped her phone for an identical model so that it would fit in her phone holder. He must have spent time in her company when she was exercising to know this.'

'You say 'he', couldn't the killer be a woman strong enough to carry the victim?'

The psychologist looked at him repugnantly. 'I know he is male because he partially removed her clothing.'

'But a woman could do the same.'

'He wanted to show his power over her. To expose her, to denigrate her. He probably took his time looking at her. He may have taken photographs with her phone or another phone or camera.'

'Why did he leave her face down if he wanted to expose and denigrate her?'

'He became embarrassed at her watching him. He probably pleasured himself there.'

'What does he do for a living?'

'He's clever, he has done his research, he knows about forensics. He's a white-collar professional, has an office job, familiar with IT. He gets his fitness from exercise, not from work, he uses a gym.

'He lives in the area, as he was familiar with it and comfortable enough to commit the murder where he did. Also, he knew the deceased recently as it was a two-year old model of phone she used and he swapped it for the exact same model. This tells us that he has a well-paid job with spare cash to spend on a phone costing a few hundred pounds.'

'Anything else?'

'He's going to be difficult to find unless he has made a mistake you've yet to find.'

* * *

Over the next few days and weeks, the CID team began to build a picture of Charlee Bucher's last few hours. It was monotonous work involving hundreds of interviews of sex offenders, her work colleagues, students, gym users, neighbours, friends and family. Reviews of CCTV, doorbell and dashcam footage, ANPR, accounts, social media and more as a digital examination of her life.

Although monotonous work, it had produced some results. Charlee Butcher had left work on the Monday, returned home and shortly afterwards gone for a run. She had been wearing her purple athletic outfit and phone on her left upper arm.

The CID team had picked her up on various bits of CCTV footage from her home in Embleton until she took a footpath into the countryside. Her phone then pinged off masts and they were able to track her route for a while. It became less accurate as she ran further away from multiple masts in Embleton and into rural Northumberland.

The attack site was known, as was the murder location. They had calculated the attack time to within a few minutes based on the speed she had been covering the ground. After the murder, they knew that her phone had been taken and replaced with another. Her original phone had remained active for approximately ten minutes and must have moved because it had pinged a telecommunications mast nearer to Embleton. The original owner of the replacement phone was identified. However, they had lost the phone and with it the trail went cold.

Less progress had been made on her life outside of work. Her work laptop had been used exclusively for work. The investigation learnt what they could of her life carried out digitally from accounts that she had held. No evidence existed that she had a tablet or laptop of her own and it looked like she conducted all her private life communications through her missing phone. Finding it was vital.

Through the hard but careful work of the FLO's they had learnt that her parents had hoped she would marry and have children. Unfortunately for them, she had married her job instead. In the early part of her career, she had told them about her work. Since gaining promotion to business manager, she talked less about her work due to the confidential nature of it. The reality was she probably didn't want her parents to know how she ruthlessly destroyed people's careers and lives.

Vicky and Elaine, her friends from university, confirmed much the same. Work and gym were her life. She occasionally would mention a man she was dating, but she had become cautious in saying too much over the years having had her hopes dashed in the past.

At first, the CID team had been hopeful that the gym would provide the clue they needed to find the killer. However, most gym members had alibis and no links were identified to be possible reasons for murder.

The list of possible suspects with motive was long if you considered all the people she had been involved in dismissing or forcing out of the university. However, one case stood out from the rest. It was the recent case which had involved Dr Elfyn Williams, Dr Bear Lawrence and five students. What made it conspicuous was that the university had never before attempted to take on two members of staff at one time in this manner. It seemed their preference was normally to isolate staff and treat them individually.

All of the students had alibis. Most were either at home, playing sport or in the pub, with numerous eye witnesses. Regardless, what motive would they have to murder Charlee Butcher? Their beef was with Dr Williams and Dr Lawrence.

Dr Williams had been working for English Heritage at Chesters Roman Fort on the day of the murder. Several eye witnesses confirmed him leaving there at about 4 pm. He had stopped for fuel close to his home, confirmed by both ANPR and CCTV, which was too far from the murder site for him to have possibly been the killer.

Dr Bear Lawrence had no clear alibi and admitted to hating Charlee Butcher for what she had done to him. In many ways he fitted the psychological profile of the killer. Male, competent with IT, in a white-collar job as a university lecture, 5'8", so not tall, but tall enough to have committed the murder. To his interviewers he looked normal and they had no reason to believe he wasn't strong enough to have committed the murder, despite his protestations.

He claimed that he was chronically ill with both myalgic encephalomyelitis (ME) and fibromyalgia. His alibi was that he was home, resting on the couch due to fatigue and pain, symptoms of these illnesses. His partner claimed she was home with him but neither had any proof to back this up. His neighbours could not confirm his being home or otherwise, but they did attest to his general lack of activity outside of the house since becoming ill. No evidence was found that put him anywhere other than at home, but that did not exclude the possibility that he was the killer.

Two members of staff involved in the case, Dr Carlang and Natasha Horseman, were now deceased. Dr Carlang had died in hospital from a heart attack and he had thickening of his heart walls. The circumstances of his death were not considered to be suspicious by the medical team treating him. Natasha Horseman had committed suicide according to the coroner. Both of these untimely cases had been reviewed but did not seem suspicious. The only murder appeared to be that of Charlee Butcher.

With so little progress, DI Morter gained DCI Alexanderson's approval to make a reconstruction of events. This was shown on the monthly national crime show, Crime Scene. Despite a flood of calls, little further progress was made in the investigation.

Chapter 12 – Budgeting

It was now several months since the body of Charlee Butcher had been found. Despite the extensive, rigorous investigation, all leads had gone cold. DCI Alexanderson had asked DI Morter to come to a meeting in his office. 'Mick, I cannot fault the work of you and your team over the last months. However, as you know, it is looking increasingly unlikely that we will solve this case. Unfortunately, I am under severe budgeting pressures and I cannot keep pouring resources into this investigation'

The jaw line of DI Morter stiffened. 'Sir, if I may be so bold, our interviews have clearly shown that the staff of Embleton University are frightened by all of this. By 'all of this', I include the deaths of Dr Carlang and Natasha Horseman together with the murder of Charlee Butcher. It's my opinion that the force needs to reassure the local population that we are doing what we can to keep them safe.'

DCI Alexanderson looked down and nodded slightly. He was hoping to let DI Morter believe he was contemplating his words. Truth was, he had given this matter much thought and was about to offer a lifeline to the investigation. 'You are right, of course you are. We have a duty to protect and serve. But I also have to consider delivering our duty efficiently and within budget. How do I resolve pouring money into this investigation to reassure a few academics when most of the wider population of Northumberland and the Cheviots are worried about knife crime, drugs, burglary and everything else?'

DI Morter clenched his fists in frustration.

'Well, I have a suggestion for you,' continued DCI Alexanderson. 'You remember that I pointed you in the direction of Charlee Butcher being the victim and also the particular issue of Dr's Williams and Lawrence at the university?

'Yes, I certainly do. I was wondering how you knew this, but thought better than to ask.'

'You will remember that Professor Robbie Mustoe was the line manager of Dr Elfyn Williams and Dr Bear Lawrence.'

DI Morter nodded in agreement.

'Well, it just so happens that Professor Mustoe is an old friend of DCI Parrish.'

'DCI Parrish? The DCI Parrish?'

'The very same. Professor Mustoe was concerned something wasn't right with the deaths of Dr Carlang and Natasha Horseman and he got in touch with Parrish even before the disappearance of Charlee Bucher. They got in touch with me via my predecessor, Andy Thompson. It was Mustoe who suspected something was wrong when Charlee Butcher failed to attend a meeting that she was supposed to be at with him. Parrish alerted me that she was possibly missing. That's why I pointed the investigation in her direction even though I had checked and knew she wasn't a misper.'

'You'd told me about what had happened with Dr's Williams and Lawrence, but I had no idea about DCI Parrish being involved.'

'Well, I gave the DCI Parrish matter some thought.'

'I'm not sure I follow, Sir. What do you mean by the DCI Parrish matter?'

'Andy Thompson has no interest in returning to active duty, golf is his thing these days. Plus, I couldn't justify the consultancy budget even if he had been interested. DCI Parrish is interested in the investigation and is keen to be involved. However, it's common knowledge that he was given early retirement because of his health issues. I thought it too risky to bring him into an early-stage full-on murder case, given his health.'

Alexanderson paused as he got ready to reveal his plan to his junior colleague. 'However, we're beyond that now. Perhaps we could invite him to look over the case now we've completed the hard yards and been unable to identify the killer? I wouldn't be able to bring him in as a consultant for financial reasons, but I could justify covering reasonable expenses for a week or two. How do you feel about that?'

'How do I feel about that? Bloody hell, Sir, if you'll forgive my French, who wouldn't take the opportunity to work with a legend like DCI Parrish.'

'Well, what are you waiting for?'

'Sir?'

'Give the man a bloody phone call, if you don't mind my French!'

* * *

Parrish ignored the call on his mobile phone as the number wasn't in his phonebook. A minute later a text arrived from the same number.

Hi DCI Parrish, this is DI Morter from Northumberland and Cheviots CID. I'm the lead investigator on the Charlee Butcher case. Please would you give me a call back on this number when it is convenient? Regards, Mick

Not wanting to sound too keen, Parrish attempted not to ring immediately. So, he fetched a glass of water from the kitchen before sitting comfortably in his Chesterfield recliner. He knew that once he made the call, he'd be walking involuntarily around his living room with his phone clasped to his head. He had to try and pace himself, not expending too much energy by not walking round in circles.

DI Morter was equally keen to speak but not show it and deliberately counted to five slowly before answering his mobile, which he could see was DCI Parrish calling.

'DI Morter speaking.'

'Hi, It's Mr Parrish returning your call.'

'Thank you for ringing back DCI Parrish.'

'Please call me P or Mr P, I'm retired these days and no longer DCI Parrish.'

'Well, I shall do my best Mr P but it's a little difficult having known of you as DCI Parrish for all these years. Do you mind me explaining the Charlee Butcher case?'

'Of course not, I'd be delighted to hear what you have to say.'

With that, DI Morter gave Parrish a precis of the case. He then outlined their offer for him to look into the case for one or two weeks, with reasonable expenses covered. Mick offered to book Parrish into a local hotel for the following week if he was free and agreeable to assisting them.

'I'd be delighted to help and I'm free next week. Unless things have changed, should I meet you at HQ about noon, so that you can get your Monday morning meetings out of the way?'

DI Morter smiled. DCI Parrish might be retired but he had lost none of his understanding of the machinations of police routine. 'Noon would be just fine. I'll reserve a parking space for a DCI Parrish, DCI carries more weight than Mr at police HQ.'

'That's fine. Just one thing though. Do you mind if I make my own hotel reservations? With my health as it is, I need to make sure the accommodation is suitable for me; not too far to walk, not too many steps, walk-in shower and so on.'

'Of course not, as long as you don't book yourself into the Ritz, I might have trouble getting the expenses approved!'

'Of course, and in the event the only suitable accommodation is more than your budget can cover, I'd happily pay the extra myself.'

'Sounds like a plan. I'll see you Monday at HQ, sometime around noon.'

'Looking forward to it, goodbye.'

'Goodbye, Mr P.'

Parrish hadn't been in such a good mood in quite literally, years. Although he had to make enquiries into accommodation, he had the urge to ring his old friend Professor Mustoe first.

'Scratcher, great to hear from you!'

'Hi Robbie, I had to ring, I have news!'

'Go on, sounds exciting.'

'I'm coming to see you next week.' With that, Parrish explained how he had been invited to look into the Charlee Butcher case and would be staying in a hotel somewhere in Embleton. It needed to be suitable for him, convenient for both the police HQ and the university in Embleton, and fall within budget. 'Perhaps you know of somewhere suitable?'

'I can help you with that.'

'Where do you recommend?'

'Our house. You'll be staying with Christine and I.'

'Are you sure? That would be wonderful.'

'Of course. You are welcome to come and go as you please.'

'Do you have a garage?'

'We do and we could fit a motorbike in there too!'

'Splendid! Would it be OK if I came down Sunday afternoon or evening?'

'Anytime to suit you, Scratcher. I'll be home and we can eat once you're settled in.'

Chapter 13 – Northumberland and Cheviots Police HQ

Christine, Robbie and Parrish had enjoyed a pleasant evening catching up. All three of them had sensibly agreed on an early night. Christine and Robbie had work in the morning and Parrish was visiting police HQ. Left to their own devices, Robbie and Parrish had a penchant for red wine and port, which could leave them somewhat diminished the following day.

It was late Monday morning when after cruising past the visitor car parking at Northumberland and Cheviots Police HQ, Parrish decided to park his Honda Forza 350 in the space reserved for bicycles. The visitor parking was for cars and offered nothing substantial to lock his scooter to, whereas stainless steel hoops embedded into the ground were available for bicycles.

With the scooter secured with a heavy chain and padlock, Parrish stored his helmet, gloves and jacket in the cavernous space under the scooter seat. Then he walked the few steps to the large glass entrance and made his way to the reception desk.

The receptionist glowered as she admonished him, 'You can't park there, that's reserved for bicycles.'

Parrish ignored her comment, 'I'm DCI Parrish, here to see DI Morter.'

The receptionist blushed slightly, 'Please take a seat DCI Parrish. I'll call him right away.'

'Thank you,' said Parrish, as he turned on his heel and made his way to the seating area.

Within minutes, DI Morter entered the reception area through a pair of security doors and made his way to the reception desk. There he completed an entry in the visitor's book and took a visitor pass hung on a dark blue lanyard from the receptionist.

DI Morter shook Parrish's hand warmly and passed him the lanyard, 'DCI Parrish, good to see you and welcome to our HQ. I'm DI Mick Morter.'

'Thank you,' said Parrish, donning the pass over his head. 'Should we?' and he gestured towards the doors, where DI Morter had appeared one minute earlier.

DI Morter suggested that they try Parrish's pass to unlock the doors and then led the way to a nearby lift, which they took up to the second floor. There they walked to the end of the corridor and entered an investigation room. Parrish immediately realised by the small size of the room that the investigation had been scaled back substantially.

The walls were covered in pictures of Charlee Butcher, both in life and death. Various details, including where she was attacked initially and where she was murdered, were on the walls. The rock used to hit her was pictured, as were the microscopic images of the coloured fibres left from the ligature on the skin of her neck. Elsewhere were lists and diagrams of names and places, maps with highlighted routes, times and dates, all trying to make sense of her life and contacts in order to find the killer. DI Morter remained silent whilst Parrish perused the room to get a feel for the case.

When they sat down, DI Morter presented the case using a slick presentation that he had obviously given previously. For the most part, Parrish remained silent, only asking the occasional question for clarification. They were interrupted briefly by Parrish's phone chiming to alert him to take another painkiller. A jug of water and a glass on the table allowed him to take the tablet. When DI Morter finished, he sat silent once again, waiting for the great man to further proceedings.

'Back in the day, I would have visited every one of these locations,' said Parrish pointing to the walls. 'However, I'm not as mobile or as full of beans as I was. Perhaps, I could have access to your database so that I can view things at my leisure from the comfort of a chair?'

DI Morter patted a laptop case on the desk. 'This is for you, whilst you are on the case. Inside are a laptop and a sheet of paper with your temporary login details. You'll have to change the password when you first log on. Why don't we do that now, so I can show you how to navigate the database?'

The two men then spent the next half hour exploring the database and the case, as Parrish got up to speed using the laptop and navigating his way through the data. Parrish was particularly interested in some of the drone footage, something that he had only limited experience with from his time in the Met.

Eventually, Parrish sat back in his chair. 'The drone footage and the videos of various locations are very interesting and useful to me given my lack of mobility. Certainly, the attack site and murder location would be inaccessible to me in my current health. Despite my limitations though, I am particularly keen to visit a few locations.'

'I'll do my best, where were you thinking?'

'The university for a start. I'd like to visit the HR department and Charlee Butcher's office in particular.'

'I can arrange that. Would tomorrow be OK?'

'That would be just fine, thanks.'

With that, DI Morter rang Heledd Morgan, the Director of HR at Embleton University.

'DI Morter,' answered Heledd frostily.

'Good afternoon, Miss Morgan,' said an over-cheery DI Morter, who enjoyed the inconvenience his investigations caused her. 'I'd like to arrange a low-key view of HR tomorrow morning by my colleague, DCI Parrish, if that wouldn't be too inconvenient for you?'

'Tell him to report to the Queen's Lodge reception at 8 am,' said Heledd immediately. She hoped to get the viewing completed before most of the staff and the majority of the students were on campus.

'8 am,' mouthed DI Morter to Parrish, covering the microphone of his phone with his hand.

Parrish replied loudly to Mick, so that Heledd Morgan would hear. 'No earlier than 10 and preferably 11 am. I have tablets to take and a morning routine to follow for my health these days. Also, I'll need transport on site, a golf buggy, motorized wheelchair or something as I would also like a tour of the campus.'

'I'll make arrangement for him to be met at main security at 11 am with suitable transport available.' Retorted Heledd in DI Morter's ear. With that, she abruptly ended the call.

'She's all charm. You'll enjoy meeting her, if your paths cross tomorrow,' smirked DI Morter.

Chapter 14 – Blue, green or rainbow?

The following morning, Parrish locked his Honda to some railings near the main security office of Embleton University. He locked away his waxed jacket and helmet after removing an aluminium folding walking stick from the under-seat storage.

Strictly speaking, he didn't need a stick to walk, although it was useful when he needed to stand and rest. ME and fibromyalgia are hidden disabilities and sometimes Parrish found it useful to make them visible with a stick. He carried a stick when he thought he might be visiting a busy area. People saw a walking stick and assumed that a person was elderly, disabled or injured in some way. Consequently, they tended to give the person room and not barge past like they may have been inclined to do.

Dressed in his nearly new Levi jeans and a pink short-sleeved Oxford shirt, Parrish considered himself to be what passed for smart and casual these days. He walked the short distance from his scooter to security accompanied by the taps of his walking stick. As punctual as ever, at exactly 11 am he reported at the security desk and they were expecting him.

'Barney, your special guest has arrived,' said the first security guard warmly.

Barney got up from his chair, where he had been watching a monitor displaying a number of live CCTV feeds. He was a very big man, both tall and broad, and looked capable of running through a locked door. His upright posture as he walked towards Parrish increased his presence even further. *Ex-military* thought Parrish to himself.

'Good morning DCI Parrish, I'm Barney, nice to meet you. Would you sign the guest register please?' As Parrish filled in the register, Barney asked him, 'what colour lanyard would you like today?'

'What are the choices?'

'University blue, green or rainbow,' replied Barney.

'I'm feeling colourful today, I'll go for rainbow please,' smiled Parrish.

With that, Barney picked a new rainbow lanyard from a box below the counter, clicked a guest pass on to it and handed it to Parrish. 'If you would wait just out front, I'll be along in a second with transport.'

'Thank you, Sir,' replied Parrish.

Within a minute, Barney drove up silently on an electric golf buggy sporting the Embleton University emblem and as many straplines and clichés as the bodywork could fit. 'Zero emission green campus transport', 'Diversity and Inclusion', 'Invest in YOUR Future' and 'Discover the best you at Embleton University' being just some of the tag lines.

'I've been told that you are a special guest and that you would like to see our HR department today,' said Barney as Parrish climbed aboard next to him.

'Well, I'm not sure I deserve to be a special guest, but I would like a tour and to see the HR department, if that would be OK?'

'You will understand, I hope, that certain parts of the university are strictly off-limits, for example due to the nature of the research. Other than those, I should be able to let you have a good look at the university.'

'Thank you, Barney. May I ask what time you started today?'

Barney looked at him quizzically, '6 am.'

'Have you had anything to eat yet, perhaps we could have a brew and a bite to eat?'

'If that's what you want, your bidding is my command.' With that, Barney squeezed the accelerator pedal and pointed the buggy towards the staff restaurant. Parrish sat holding a grab handle to steady himself and smiled at the thought that he had lost none of his detective ability. He was befriending Barney, who Parrish assumed to be ex-military and had guessed correctly to have started a shift before the campus awoke. Over some food and a hot drink, Parrish would quiz Barney to get the word on the ground on the comings and goings at the university. Heledd Morgan had unwittingly helped the enquiry more than she had intended.

Parrish asked some inane questions to begin with; how big was the university? How many students were there? All predictable stuff that he expected a security guard trusted to give tours to special guests to know. Then he shifted his questions to Barney to show an interest in him; how long had he worked at the university? Had he always worked in security here and crucially, what had he done before he joined the university?

True to expectations, Barney had been in the Green Howards, an infantry regiment of the British Army. He had seen action in the Bosnian conflict and Northern Ireland. Deliberately leaning towards Barney, Parrish wanted his body language to show fascination and admiration for Barney and his military career.

Feeling that he had gained Barney's trust to some extent, Parrish returned to his visit and suggested a trip to HR after they had finished in the canteen. Naturally, this wasn't a problem, so Parrish asked what other sights they might take in on their way to HR, which Barney then described.

Previously, Parrish had looked at a map of the university and had already planned the first stop at the staff restaurant. The natural path from the canteen to HR would take them past several university buildings including the Geography building, where Dr Carlang had been based. When Barney mentioned the Geography building, Parrish took his opportunity.

'Do you think we might stop to take a look at where Dr John Carlang had worked and his office?' asked Parrish.

Barney looked puzzled, which briefly concerned Parrish. 'Which office do you mean?'

Thinking on his feet, Parrish asked, 'all of them?'

'Sure thing. We can stop by his office in Geography and then take a look at his office in HR,' replied Barney, 'although the offices may be reallocated now.'

This is gold dust, thought Parrish to himself. He hadn't suspected that Dr Carlang had another office other than in Geography. He also couldn't recall any mention or pictures from the police database for Dr Carlang either in Geography or HR. In fact, he now realised that no mention had been made in the database about either Dr Carlang or Natasha Horseman. 'Did you know Dr Carlang?' asked Parrish as nonchalantly as possible.

'More by reputation than anything else.'

'And what reputation was that?'

'Usually harmless, but also one to avoid upsetting,' replied Barney.

Not wanting to push his luck, Parrish left the questioning there for now. This was turning into a very useful tour of the university.

They left the buggy parked at the steps to the entrance to the Geography building. Geography was housed in a concrete monstrosity built in the 1960's, which would have managed to look both contemporary and futuristic at that time.

The Personnel Department, as HR was known back then, had been the first occupants of the building. After Personnel moved to a newer building, Maths had moved in. After Maths later moved to another newer build, Geography had been upgraded from a building built between the Great Wars.

Such was the hierarchy at Embleton, the Personnel and later HR, carried more power than most academic departments. This was because they were instrumental in promotions and implementing the wishes of the highest post-holders of the university. Their ability to pick and choose occupancy of the newest building was symptomatic of their power. HR feasted at the top table, whereas Geography fed on scraps.

Once inside the lobby of the Geography building, Barney and Parrish took a lift to the fourth floor, where Barney knew Dr Carlang had had an office. Barney led the way along the corridor to where the office had been.

The office door had a rectangular patch where a sign had previously been, presumably saying 'Dr John Carlang'. The door was locked and through the window it could be seen that the office had been redecorated and was empty, save for a desk, lamp, bin, book shelves, a leather chair behind the desk and six plastic chairs with their backs against the wall opposite the desk.

'Do you think we could go in?' asked Parrish.

'Probably, but why, there's nothing to see here?'

'I want to get a feel for the place, take a look out of the window, listen to the background noise.'

Barney suggested that Parrish wait at the office to save him walking further than necessary. Then he went to reception. Barney had a master key with which he could have gained access, but he chose to be diplomatic. At reception, the secretary on duty was about to fetch a key to the office, when Barney explained he had a master key. She asked him to lockup after he had been in and turned back to her work.

Back at the office, Barney unlocked the door and they both went in. The room smelt of fresh paint and carpet cleaner. With the door closed, the external noise was minimal, which Parrish had expected. Lecturers regularly held confidential meetings with staff and students and would not want to be overheard. The view was unremarkable other than from being on the fourth floor, much of the campus could be seen.

'Where are all his books, his computer, personal effects?' asked Parrish.

'Any computer equipment belongs to the university and would have been returned to the IT department. The contents of his desk, any pictures, mugs, pens, stationary would have been put in a box for his next of kin to collect. Likewise, the books and papers, although these often go uncollected. The academics and students then rifle through them, taking anything of interest, whatever is left goes in the skip.'

'Is it usual for staff to have more than one office?'

'It's not unusual but it's not common either. The university has projects that involve multiple departments, which usually results in some duplication of offices for staff.'

'Is it unusual for staff to have an office in HR and another elsewhere?'

Barney thought for a moment. 'Good question. I can't think of anyone, other than Dr Carlang and Pro Vice-Chancellor, Professor Vince Cook who have an office in HR and another office elsewhere.'

'Professor Vince Cook?'

'You didn't hear this from me, right. Word was that Dr Carlang wrote reports for HR about staff and students the university wanted rid of. PVC chaired the meetings that got rid of them.'

Parrish made an unreliable mental note to check out PVC, as he was known. 'Shall we move on to HR?'

'Of course. Let's make our way down to the buggy.'

It was no more than two minutes in the buggy to the Queen's Lodge building where HR was now housed. The contrast with the Geography building was stark. Built within the last ten years, Queen's Lodge was a glass and steel behemoth. As was typical, HR had been allowed to bag one floor by the university top brass, despite many academic departments desperate for more modern accommodation.

Barney parked the buggy close to the large glass doors to the building. Inside was an ultra-modern reception area furnished with stylish contemporary seating and coffee tables laden with university promotional brochures where guests could wait. And wait they must. Entry to the inner echelons of the building required guests to report to the large curved reception desk. If they were on the daily visitors list, they would be issued guest passes and offered a choice of lanyards, as Parrish had witnessed earlier, before being asked to take a seat. Persons not on the list, would be invited to both leave their details and the building.

To gain entry through a second set of glass doors, guests would have to wait to be collected by an authorised person to accompany them. HR were not popular amongst staff and wanted protection from anybody wishing to force themselves inside, with or without warning.

Whilst Barney and Parrish waited, an alarm on the phone in Parrish's pocket chimed. He took it out and cancelled the alarm. From his opposite pocket he took out a strip of tablets as he walked over to a water cooler. He washed the painkiller down with a few sips of chilled water and returned to his seat.

Parrish didn't have to wait long to be collected by Rachel Sturridge from the HR team. Barney got up out of his chair to join them.

'Would you mind waiting here for me please, Barney?'

'Of course not.'

'In fact, as I'm not sure how long I will be, why don't I ring security when I'm ready to be collected so that you are free to do whatever you want?'

'I've got my orders, Sir. I'll be waiting here for you when you are done, no problem.'

'That's very kind, thank you Barney.'

Rachel and Parrish walked to the lift. Adopting his usual modus operandi, Parrish attempted to befriend his latest guide, thanking her for the forthcoming tour. Typically, he asked questions to reassure her of his ostensibly benign nature and listened to what Rachel had to say and what useful information she might reveal.

As Rachel and Parrish took the lift to the fifth floor, where HR were based, Parrish considered who his guide was. Rachel Sturridge appeared to be in her forties. She was smartly dressed with a neat hair style and was wearing both an engagement and wedding ring on fingers with painted nails.

Pictures and knowledge he had of Heledd Morgan and Charlee Butcher revealed them to be both driven, career women, single, extremely well-dressed, with both manicured hair and nails.

Parrish imagined that Rachel was experienced in HR, with a degree of responsibility but not in a management post. Heledd Morgan had probably chosen her to be his guide today as she was considered a safe pair of hands.

Exiting the lift and going through yet another set of doors requiring an authorised pass to open them,

Rachel led Parrish into the HR department. 'Where would you like to start?' asked Rachel in her local accent.

'Why not here? Perhaps you could tell me what we're looking at and a little about the department?'

As she talked, Parrish studied the room silently. The architects and designers had worked their magic to make the space feel light and airy with the use of large expanses of glass and sophisticated lighting. However, Parrish knew from bitter experience that this was a temperature and humidity-controlled environment.

Working in such places in the past had made him miserable and often ill. Germs were allowed to spread amongst the occupants in what he thought of as fetid air. It was exactly this type of environment where he had caught a viral infection, which had led to him becoming chronically ill with ME and fibromyalgia.

Most of the department was open plan with seating for thirty to forty people, estimated Parrish. There was also a large networked printer. To one side, an open door revealed a small kitchen. The open plan area had windows on both sides allowing in natural light. At each end of the room, as well as the kitchen, were offices and meeting rooms which all had a single glass wall on the side facing the main office.

Rachel explained that the open plan area was where most of the people in HR worked, supporting the three faculties. 'Did Natasha Horseman work in here?'

Rachel looked a little surprised by the question but answered, 'yes, she sat at the empty desk in the back row, second from the right.'

Parrish nodded slightly and said no more as they stood in silence and he continued to look around the room.

All the staff in the main office were female, except for one man. This contrasted with what he had witnessed so far on his tour. Another striking difference was that every member of staff wore a rainbow lanyard, unlike the mixed choice of lanyards he had seen before. Parrish very tactfully addressed the lanyards. 'When I arrived today, I was given a choice of lanyards, university blue, green, and rainbow which I chose. So far on my tour of the university, I've seen staff wearing all three colours of the lanyard, but here everyone is wearing a rainbow lanyard. I'm curious as to why this is, department policy perhaps?'

'Every member of the university, both student and staff are free to express themselves without censorship, within the boundaries of the law, obviously. As such, staff can choose to wear whatever lanyard they wish to. Diversity and inclusion are also at the heart of what we do and who we are at Embleton. HR pride ourselves on that and choose to wear the rainbow lanyard.'

'Very impressive,' lied Parrish. *What tripe*, he thought, *probably de facto policy coming from Heledd Morgan forcing her staff to wear rainbow lanyards.*

Whilst they chatted, Parrish had also been taking in the offices. Two rooms were larger than the others, one lit, one unlit. In the lit room, Parrish could see a woman working at a desk, who looked like Heledd Morgan from a photo he had seen. It being one of the largest offices, Parrish deduced that this was indeed Heledd.

Although unlit, Parrish could see that the other large room contained a large table surrounded by chairs. He pigeon-holed this in his mind as the HR meeting room.

Now concentrating on the smaller offices, Parrish counted six of them. Four were lit with people working in them, two were in darkness. Of the four offices drizzled with light, three were occupied my women and one by a stern looking, well-dressed man, probably in his fifties. Pondering this information, Parrish thought that it was possible that he was looking at the three business managers for each faculty. *And could the man be PVC*, he wondered?

Rachel was patiently waiting for Parrish to ask something. With his finely tuned social skills, Parrish obliged by beginning to probe for information. 'I hope you don't mind my taking a guess here? Would that be Heledd Morgan in the large office on the far left-and side?'

'Yes, it is, she's the Director of HR.'

'Then we have those three ladies in the office towards the right-hand side. Might they be the faculty business managers?'

'I'm impressed, DCI Parrish.'

'There is a distinguished-looking gentlemen in one of the offices. Am I looking at the Pro Vice-Chancellor?' Brain fog had caused his memory to partially fail him. He could remember that this man was nicknamed PVC, but he could only recall his title, Pro Vice-Chancellor.

'We're looking at one of the Pro Vice-Chancellor's. There are several Pro V-Cs in the university at any one time.'

Silence descended between Rachel and Parrish. He sensed she was starting to clam up by not revealing the identity of this Pro V-C. Never mind, he would keep on probing for information and knew he might soon have to push for answers.

'That leaves the large meeting room and two empty offices. One of those presumably belonged to the late Charlee Butcher?'

'Yes, one of those was her office,' said Rachel sadly.

'I'm very sorry for your loss. As you know, I am investigating her case and hoping to get justice by capturing her killer. Please may we take a look in her office?'

Without words, Rachel led the way to what was Charlee Butcher's office. She opened the door, which was unlocked and turned on the lights. Similarly, to Dr Carlang's office in the Geography building, this office had been freshly cleaned and the walls painted. The office contained only a desk, lamp, four chairs; a leather one for Charlee behind the desk and three for visitors, a bin and a modern wooden locking filling cabinet.

Parrish closed the door behind them before slowly walking around the room. He was looking carefully, smelling the scent of the air, listening intently and gently touching, almost caressing the few objects in the room as if they could speak to him through his fingertips. The filing cabinet had keys in the lock, so he unlocked it only to find all the drawers were empty.

He sat down in what had been her chair and gestured to Rachel to sit opposite him, which she did slowly and apparently reluctantly. 'I don't wish to upset you, so please take your time. Would you tell me what Charlee was like?'

Rachel looked upset and annoyed. 'We've all answered this question several times since the murder. Do we really have to go through this again?'

'No, we don't. I apologise,' said Parrish to appease her. 'There is a kitchen in the corner of the main office. Do people drink their tea or coffee in there at break times?'

'Gosh, we weren't asked that before. I suppose it depends, either there or at your desk. I grab something to drink when I reach a natural break in my work. Usually, I'd ask colleagues sat near me if they would like me to make them something.'

'Sounds perfectly normal, just like in a police station. And what happens at lunchtime?'

'Some people head in to town to get lunch, go to the bank, go shopping, you know how it is. Others eat at their desk or go to the staff restaurant. Just depends on what you need to do.'

He nodded in agreement. She was back on track. Now to start asking some questions that might reveal more. 'Do the people who have an office use the kitchen as those people do in the main office?'

'Yes, well, sort of. I'd say they spend more time at their desks and are less inclined to chat.'

'But they do still chat with their colleagues sometimes?'

'Certainly. Particularly if you're at the kitchen boiling the kettle or whatever, when they come to use the kitchen, they would usually say hello and chat.'

'About work or more casual stuff?'

'Well, they do both, but some are more work-orientated than others.'

'From what I know about Charlee Butcher, she was very focused on her career.'

'Yes, she was, quite a private person. She might ask what I was doing at the weekend, but I got the feeling she was doing it out of politeness. If I asked her the same, she gave little away. She would say, 'probably go for a run, go to the gym, watch a movie', you know the sort of thing.'

'I do indeed. I've been guilty of that myself in the past, focused on my career and not enough on my family and friends.'

Rachel nodded in understanding. Now for a question to move his investigation on a bit. 'What about Dr Carlang?'

Rachel faltered a little. 'What about Dr Carlang?'

'Did he chat at the kitchen over a drink? Was he a private person or more open?'

Rachel looked unsure as to what to say. This was not a line of questioning from any of the previous detectives. She was brought up by her parents to be truthful, especially when talking to a policeman and she felt compelled to answer. 'Er, yes, he would chat over a coffee. He was quite an open person.'

'Did he talk about his work?'

Again, she faltered, unsure of how to answer the question. 'He never talked about work. I'm not sure what he did really.'

'His office was next to the Pro V-C's, wasn't it?'

'He had an office in Geography.'

'And he had an office here to, didn't he?'

She couldn't put off answering his question any longer. 'Yes, he did.'

'I'd like to take a look please.'

Eager to avoid answering any more questions, she led Parrish to the former office of Dr Carlang in HR. But before she could enter, Parrish stopped her. 'Have the police examined this room before?'

'Not that I know of.'

Parrish peered through the glass wall into the office. It looked exactly like Charlee Butcher's office, cleaned and ready for a new occupant, except for a cardboard packing box on the floor in the corner. 'What is in the box?'

'It's the personal effects of Dr Carlang.'

'So, they haven't been collected?'

'Not so far.'

'He passed away a few months ago, it's a bit unusual that they haven't been collected yet, isn't it?' He was thinking aloud and stopped talking when he realised what he was doing. 'Can we take a seat in the meeting room please?' asked Parrish.

'Certainly,' said Rachel and she then led them both to the meeting room, where they sat with the lights now turned on. They both sat quietly whilst Parrish thought. He deliberately adopted a pose massaging his temple to emphasize that he was thinking and wanted to be left to his thoughts.

Dr Carlang's personal effects had been removed from his office in Geography, but not from his office in HR. Was it all just an after-thought? If the contents were that important, would someone not have thought to pass them on to his next of kin? Equally, if these items were that important, why had they not been stored or even destroyed to hide something? Could this be linked to his death, Charlee Butcher's murder or even Natasha Horseman's death?

'You said earlier that you didn't know what Dr Carlang did.'

'That's correct.'

'But you could see him in his office.'

'Of course.'

'So did you see him spend time with other colleagues?'

'Like I said, he would chat over a coffee.'

'Did he spend time with Charlee Butcher, that you could see?' asked Parrish, more forcefully.

'Yes,' replied Rachel with some discomfort.

'Did he spend time with the Pro V-C?'

'Yes.'

'Heledd Morgan?'

'Sometimes. We all did occasionally.' Rachel was flustered by the questioning.

'But Heledd didn't spend much time with Dr Carlang or the Pro V-C?'

'Not often.'

'Did you see Charlee Butcher, Dr Carlang and the Pro V-C together regularly?'

'Yes,' said Rachel defiantly.

Parrish turned slightly, looked away from Rachel, pulled out his mobile and dialled.

'How was the tour?' asked DI Morter.

'I'm still at the university. I've just been in Dr Carlang's office in HR'.

'But Dr Carlang was based in Geography.'

'And he also had an office in HR, just a few yards from Charlee Butcher's office and the desk of Natasha Horseman. And he worked with Charlee Butcher and one of the Pro V-C's on a regular basis in HR.'

Parrish let that hang in the air for DI Morter to take in before he continued. 'I'm sat with Rachel from HR in their meeting room. She tells me that she doesn't think the police have examined Dr Carlang's office here. Do you know if SOCO have taken a look at it?'

'I know for certain that they haven't. They only looked at Charlee Butcher's office.'

'Can you get them here ASAP? There is a box in Dr Carlang's office, which contains his personal effects that need examining as well as the room. I suggest we examine the Pro V-C's room too.'

'Agreed. Are you OK to stay there until either SOCO or I arrive?'

'Of course.'

'I'll be there as soon as I can.'

The call ended, Parrish put his phone back in his pocket and turned back to look at Rachel. 'Would you be kind enough to tell Barney that I'm going to be at least half an hour more before I need a lift to main security? Also, the lead investigator on the

Charlee Butcher murder case, DI Morter, and Scene of Crime Officers are going to need access to HR as soon as they arrive at this building. I want no delay downstairs. Do you understand me?'

'Yes, of course,' nodded a shocked Rachel.

'But before you do that, the Pro V-C will have to leave his office immediately. Both his office and Dr Carlang's are off-limits now until they've been examined.'

Rachel looked mortified, nodded her understanding of his instructions and left the room in haste. From his chair, Parrish had a vantage point to see through the glass wall that she did exactly as he had dictated. With the meeting door still open, he could hear the Pro V-C loudly protesting his displeasure at being forced to leave his office. *C'est la vie*, thought Parrish, who smiled to himself.

Chapter 15 – Flat battery

DI Morter arrived within twenty minutes. He chatted to Parrish briefly in the meeting room and would have liked to have talked for longer. However, Parrish was exhausted with the day's activities, even though he had been on the university campus for less than two hours.

The energy expended on the excitement of the case was taking a toll on him, as was the physical effort of travelling from Helmsley to Embleton and visiting both the police HQ and the university. Parrish knew he desperately needed to rest and recuperate if he was to avoid a crash.

Barney was still waiting for Parrish in reception of the Queen's Lodge building when Parrish exited the lift. Rachel had offered to accompany Parrish down in the lift, but Parrish had declined the offer. He wanted no small talk, simply to get to his bed in Robbie's house as soon as possible.

The offer by Barney to tour more of the campus in the buggy was also declined by Parrish. So, they headed straight for the main security office.

'I'll fill in the paperwork for you, if you like,' offered Barney.

'That would be appreciated.'

'All I need is your pass.'

'What about the lanyard?'

'You can keep that if you want to.'

'Yes please. A little memento from my visit.'

'It's all yours. Great to meet you, DCI Parrish. If you want to visit again and complete the tour, make sure you ask for me.'

'Thank you, Barney. Good bye.' Parrish made his way slowly back to the scooter, the walking stick now proving useful in supporting him to walk. Bending down to unlock the padlock and chain was so painful he winced, as was bending his leg over the low seat to climb aboard.

It would have been sensible to leave the scooter and take a taxi back to Robbie's house. But brain fog was preventing Parrish making logical decisions. He could think of only one thing at a time, at best. Quite how he made it back without an accident was a miracle. With the scooter locked in the garage, Parrish went straight to his room, partially undressed and climbed into bed.

Sometime in the early hours of Wednesday morning, Parrish awoke feeling completely unrefreshed. He hadn't woken up when Christine and Robbie had returned home the previous evening. He was utterly exhausted, shattered, completely fatigued, nothing in the tank, or any words to that effect.

So drained of energy did he feel, that he couldn't, or wouldn't, lift his eyelids. Not a muscle was he moving, except for those that kept him alive, his beating heart and breathing lungs.

Hours passed as he lay motionless in bed. He heard and imagined Robbie and Christine wake and go through their own morning routines; taking a shower, eating breakfast, drinking coffee, checking their emails and news on their phones. Eventually, they both left for work.

Later, his phone vibrated in the pocket of his jeans. The battery was probably nearly flat and that *might be DI Morter with important information from SOCO about the case,* he thought. But all of it, every last bit of it could wait. The most important battery to recharge was his own internal one.

With what felt like a monumental effort, Parrish turned onto his side. Out of the corner of his eye he could see a glass of water and his lansoprazole, which he needed to take before he could eat and take the rest of his medication, 30 to 60 minutes later. Normally, he would note the time when he took the tablets, so that he knew when to eat. Today, he simply closed his eyes and lay motionless until he felt he had enough energy to do anything else at all.

Unaware of how much time had passed, he eventually felt that he could tackle a little food and his medication. A shower could wait, that was too much like hard work. Taking his phone from a pocket in his jeans and without looking at any messages, emails or anything else, he placed it on the cordless charger next to his bed.

Next, from his travel bag he took a small plastic container, which contained all the medication he needed to take for one morning. He made his way to the kitchen and ate a chocolate biscuit that he found in a cupboard. After using his inhaler, he swallowed all the tablets with gulps of cold water. A second puff on his inhaler and he was done. Back to bed for more rest and recovery.

A few hours later and feeling famished, he visited the kitchen again. After a microwave ready meal, another painkiller and more water, he went back to bed.

It was late afternoon, when he heard first Christine and then Robbie return home from work. Parrish picked up his phone from the charger and looked at it. He ignored every message and email and simply typed a message to DI Morter.

My battery is flat. Need to recover. Will be in touch.

After pulling on a few comfy clothes, he made the effort to see his hosts. Realising how exhausted he was, they suggested they make some food for him. Whilst he was welcome to join them to eat, chat, watch TV or whatever, they understood his need to recover if he returned to bed.

Parrish sat completely still on the sofa until the food was ready. He ate with his hosts, thanked them, then made his apologies and returned to bed. He hoped that by tomorrow he would have rested sufficiently to get back on the case.

Chapter 16 – Imminent danger to life

The next morning, Parrish woke and assessed his condition. His thighs burned like he had run a marathon and his arms were almost too heavy to lift. Normally, he would have had another rest day doing very little, but he had to at least read his messages and speak to DI Morter.

Like Groundhog Day, he washed down another lansoprazole. After waiting half an hour, he made his way to the kitchen via the bathroom. Christine and Robbie had already left. Consequently, he didn't feel safe enough to use the stove on his own. His concentration span was minimal and he was prone to getting distracted. Burning his friend's house down wouldn't be a good idea, or any other house for that matter.

The toaster and microwave were safe enough to use and he made himself his favourite, beans on toast. Orange juice from the fridge was a pleasant treat to wash down his tablets from another pre-prepared small plastic container. Two puffs of his inhaler and he was not ready to face the world, but he could at least tackle his phone.

DI Morter hadn't replied to the message Parrish had sent him, but he had sent a message prior to that.

Hi Mr P, SOCO finished at Embleton HR. Nothing remarkable so far, but three little piggies to discuss when you are ready. Mick

Parrish began to type a reply but immediately got frustrated with typing, so he rang DI Morter.

'Good morning, Mr P. Are you feeling any better?'

'Thanks for asking. Been worse, been better. Three little piggies, you say?'

'I'll get to that. Dr Carlang's office had been repainted and cleaned. No bodily fluids identified. Only a few prints on the chairs and desk top. We couldn't identify all of them, but most belonged to the cleaner who we printed and others probably from whoever painted the room, which we're still following up.

'Underneath the desk on the visitor's side were a few prints. Charlee Butcher's were there and another set. We took Professor Vince Cook's prints and got a match. Same story in his office. The desktop had likely been cleaned since Butcher and Carlang died, underneath we found their prints still. With both offices, almost all the prints were from the three little piggies, Butcher, Carlang and Cook.'

'What about the box from Dr Carlang's office?'

'Not a great deal in it. He must have been an Embleton United supporter, he had a team mug and coaster. We found his DNA and prints on both the mug and his coaster.'

Both men fell silent, Parrish thinking, Mick waiting. Eventually, DI Morter broke the silence. 'Any thoughts or suggestions?'

'I'd like to ponder what you just told me and what I saw and heard when I toured the campus. Not really been able to do that so far. The only thing I do know is I would like you to invite Rachel Sturridge from HR into the station for a chat with us both when I'm up to it.'

'Once you let me know when it's good for you, I'll make it happen. Why Rachel? Has she got something to do with this?'

'I don't think so. I think Heledd made her my guide because she was trusted. And rightly so, she was reluctant to answer some of my questions, probably out of loyalty. But she cannot tell a lie either and when pushed she answered all my questions. She may be able to help us understand how the department operates in both a social and business sense.'

'Sounds interesting. I look forward to hearing from you.'

'Hopefully, speak to you soon.' With the phone call finished, Parrish put the dirty dishes in the dishwasher and decided that he too needed a wash. He carelessly pulled his clothes off in the bedroom and wandered through to the bathroom where his hosts had left him towels.

In the bathroom, he stared into the mirror. The rainbow lanyard was still around his neck. He took it off and noticed that he had a red mark where it must have rubbed his skin.

He turned away, got in the shower and soon began to enjoy the hot water easing and soothing his muscles and skin. He looked at the array of bottles on the shelf in the shower and picked up the first shampoo he came across. With the shampoo massaged into his scalp, he began to use the lather of bubbles to wash himself. Suddenly, he felt a sharp pain on his neck where the lanyard had rubbed his skin. He shouted 'YES!' and punched the air, still stood naked in the shower.

Parrish had realised that he may have discovered the identity of the murder weapon, the ligature used to strangle Charlee Butcher – a rainbow lanyard. The pathologist had found multi-coloured fibres in the wound caused by a thin ligature when Butcher had been strangled. Both the pathologist and the police had assumed the fibres may have come from a climbing cord or rope, possibly a thin belt. But they could have come from a rainbow lanyard too and there were hundreds of them in Embleton University.

Forensic examination could confirm, or otherwise, if indeed a rainbow lanyard could be the murder weapon. *But was it significant? Had the killer chosen a rainbow lanyard deliberately, versus a university blue or green one? Also, why did all the staff wear rainbow lanyards in HR? Was it de facto policy or was it some other reason?*

HR was almost exclusively female. Why was that? Why were more men not employed? Could it be bias when employing new staff? Might it be the result of men leaving HR? Maybe specifically leaving Embleton HR as a result of the new Heledd Morgan regime?

Parrish realised he had been stood in the shower for far too long. His fingers had wrinkled. He turned the shower off and got out. DI Morter would soon be getting a call when he was dried and dressed.

'Mr P, I didn't expect to hear from you so soon, what have you got for me?'

'The murder weapon.'

'The weapon used to kill Charlee Butcher?'

'Well, yes and no. You'll need forensics to check, but I think she was strangled with a rainbow-coloured lanyard from Embleton University. I've not got THE murder weapon, but I'd bet money on it being one of those lanyards.'

'How ever did you work that out?'

'At main security you can choose a lanyard, university blue, green or rainbow. When you tour the campus, you'll see a mix of all three colours, plus others promoting companies, projects, sports and the like. In HR, everyone wears a rainbow lanyard. I've not figured out the significance of it yet, but my copper's nose tells me there is a link.'

'You're unbelievable. The reality of working with you is even better than the legend. You've been on this a couple of days and you've moved the case on and probably found the murder weapon. Stunning.'

'That's very kind, but I'm just providing a fresh pair of eyes.'

'You're too modest. Could you have the case solved by the end of the day please?' laughed DI Morter.

'I can't promise that, but I'm going to spend the rest of the day contemplating what we've learnt, doing some research and thinking of our next moves.'

'Thank you so much. I'll drive over to the university now and pick up a lanyard for forensics to examine. Let me know when you want to interview Rachel and anything else I can help you with.'

'Thank you, I'll be in touch.' Sat in the living room, Parrish broke out the laptop he had been given from Northumberland and Cheviots Police. With his latest questions running through his mind still, he Googled:

gender ratio in HR

Suggestions of other searches came up and he selected:

why most hr are female

The reason given was because women tend to be more social animals than men, thus attracting more women to the profession. He searched on, looking for gender ratio in HR. Various sources quoted values from 70% to 90%.

In the main office of Embleton HR, Parrish had seen one man and about thirty women. That was over 95% female. Even if he counted in Dr Carlang and PVC, which also meant including Heledd, Butcher and three other female business managers who all had offices, it was still over 90% female. His research had confirmed some of what he had pondered in the shower.

These were numbers, proportions, partly but not entirely factual and Parrish liked hard facts. It was reasonable to expect an HR department to be mainly, even predominantly, female. However, Embleton HR seemed disproportionally female. *Why was this, was it Heledd Morgan's influence?*

It should be possible to get the gender ratio of Embleton HR pre- and post- Heledd Morgan's appointment. These would be facts, thought Parrish. *But what if they were the same ratio? What would that indicate? A long-held disposition to employ female staff over male? Could misandry be at play here?* That was not a concept he thought would be popular to express, but he was a detective in search of the truth and had to consider the possibility.

And there was the rainbow lanyard prevalence in HR to consider too. *What did a rainbow represent?* He was pretty sure it was LGBTQ+ but he Googled it anyway. The results were slightly surprising to him. Many results talked of the bible and God, which he hadn't expected. Other results talked of diversity and inclusivity, much like the Embleton University doctrine expressed by Rachel from HR. Some of the results said a rainbow expressed Gay Pride.

He put the laptop down on the coffee table and thought about these two questions. *Why was Embleton HR staffing so female biased? Why did all of them wear a rainbow lanyard and not a mix of lanyard colours like elsewhere in the uni? Could it be as simple as the Director's unwritten directive?*

Could HR management have a misandrist, or more than one, amongst them? But the various meanings of rainbow lanyards contrasted with this? Didn't they? Was there a possibility that a rainbow lanyard could mean something else to some people? Instead of gay pride, could it mean anti-heterosexual to some? This was not a comfortable concept for Parrish, so he attempted to change tack.

Why was Charlee Butcher murdered with a rainbow lanyard? Was it that the killer simply had a rainbow lanyard to hand? Was Charlee Butcher gay and the murderer straight? Was Charlee Butcher anti-heterosexual and the killer heterosexual? Enough of the confusing possible sexual aspect, he thought. *Was the killer from HR?* His gut told him that the latter was a good shout, particularly in comparison to sexual belief possibilities, *but why murder someone from your own department? Why Charlee Butcher? What had she done to them? Did she have something they wanted? Yes, that's a possibility. Could it be that Butcher had been promoted ahead of someone?*

This conflicted with the profile of the murderer being male as almost all the staff were female. *Who were the men in HR? Dr Carlang, who died before Butcher was murdered. One man who worked in the main office, could be him. Which leaves Professor Vince Cook, not seemingly officially part of HR but who had an office there.* Parrish tapped into the laptop and database. He couldn't find an interview for the Pro V-C or any notes on him. *Had the Professor made himself scarce in the aftermath of Butcher's murder and worked from home or one of his other university offices? Definitely a suspect*, thought Parrish.

After a short break to clear his thoughts so far, he started his analysis again. *Charlee Butcher had been murdered. Dr Carlang had died in a seemingly plausible manner. Natasha Horseman had apparently committed suicide. Three people, all sat within yards of each other when they all worked in Embleton HR. But the three little piggies, as DI Morter had called them, were Butcher, Carlang and Cook.*

'Oh, my goodness!' cried Parrish. He grabbed his phone and rang DI Morter, who answered almost immediately.

'Hi Mr P, forensics are examining a lanyard as we speak.'

'I'm not ringing about that. This is urgent. You remember that Professor Robbie Mustoe first alerted me to the deaths of Carlang and Horseman?'

'Yes.'

'Well, I'm not ruling out the death of Horseman as being part of this, but more importantly, I think we need to consider the possibility that either Professor Vince Cook is the killer, or an attack on his life is imminent.'

'The Pro V-C?'

'Yes, him. The killer was male, tall, white-collar. The Pro V-C has an office, yards from where Charlee Butcher worked. The possibility exists that he may be the killer, at the very least he has to be a suspect and I can't find any record on the database of him being interviewed.'

'From memory, I can't recall him popping up on our radar, let alone being interviewed. He's not officially an HR employee, he can't be, him and Carlang were supposed to be independent in their roles, which we now know they clearly weren't. I'll make arrangements to interview him ASAP. But what about him being in danger of being murdered, that's the total opposite?'

'You called it yourself. The three little piggies, Butcher, Carlang and Cook. The fingerprints prove they worked as a team, which we had already suspected from what Professor Mustoe had told us about Dr's Williams and Lawrence. My guide, Barney, described the same on my tour and that was also confirmed by Rachel in HR. We need to consider the very real possibility that his life is in danger.'

'I'll speak to DCI Alexanderson immediately after we've finished talking. I understand your concerns, but the deaths of Dr Carlang and Horseman have already been investigated and explained. It'll be a big ask to get Cook protection on what is currently a hunch. We need something more concrete, starting with his interview and any possible alibi.'

'I'm sorry for racing ahead like this. But my instinct tells me that he is in danger.'

'I'll talk to DCI Alexanderson.'

'Let's speak tomorrow. I have more thinking to do.'

'Get some rest Mr P. I'll wait for your call.'

Chapter 17 - Elfyn vs Bear

Parrish decided to go back to bed until his hosts returned home later. Once in bed, his mind kept racing through the case. He had to stop this as it was using valuable energy. He tried to do this by imagining he was laid on a beach of hot white sand next to a beautiful blue Caribbean sea.

Footsteps in the hallway and the front door shutting firmly woke Parrish. Over the next quarter of an hour, he managed to manoeuvre very slowly from lying prone to be being dressed in comfortable relaxed clothing to spend an evening with his friends in their home.

'Hi Christine, sorry I've not been very sociable.'

'Hi P, don't apologise at all. We understand you need to rest.'

They continued to chat in the kitchen whilst Christine prepared a meal for later that evening. Robbie arrived and exchanged pleasantries with his friend before having a quick wash and a change of clothes. The three of them enjoyed wine and a delicious dinner together, chatting casually and catching up on what they had done that day.

Eventually, the subject changed to the case. Now officially on the case, albeit as a guest, Parrish was forbidden from discussing it with them. This was a problem though, as it was Robbie who had brought the deaths of Carlang and Horseman to his attention and identified that Butcher had gone missing. He elected to be open and tell them that he couldn't discuss matters. But, by way of a compromise, he decided to reveal that he had identified the murder weapon without saying what it was. Both Christine and Robbie were astounded at this development in such a short time.

'I suppose you have plans for investigative work such as forensic analysis and interviews?' asked Robbie inquisitively.

'I rather thought you might be able to help me with the latter?' said Parrish. 'I have to examine the previous lines of enquiry.'

'Which were?'

'I don't suppose I'm revealing anything I shouldn't, given that you brought this all to my attention. The list of suspects includes Elfyn Williams and Bear Lawrence. Elfyn has a cast-iron alibi, Bear doesn't in the opinion of the police. They haven't got ME and fibromyalgia like both Bear and I do. If they had, they would know he didn't do it.'

'So how do you prove he's innocent?'

'I start doing that by you telling me about both Bear and Elfyn. Everything you can tell me, good and bad, at work, outside of work, everything. I need to understand both men and how they tick.'

'Gosh. Where do I start? I have the upmost respect for both Bear and Elfyn. In so many ways, professionalism, experience and their abilities as both engineers and educators. They are in many ways so very similar, yet completely different at the same time.'

'What do you mean? In what ways?'

'They both have degrees in mechanical engineering, PhD's in biomedical engineering, years of industrial experience, research and teaching. They've both been pilots, Elfyn was an aeroplane pilot, Bear flew helicopters. To say one was better than the other in any particular aspect would be to the detriment of the other.

'Where they differ in the workplace is that Elfyn understands the corporate world, large organisations, governance and politics and can operate at any level. Bear can't fit in to such a world and he knows it. He's a sort of rogue operator, a maverick. He's at his best running his own companies or working for himself. I wanted his talents at Embleton University and he only agreed to do so under certain conditions.'

'Such as?' asked Parrish curiously.

'He wouldn't work Mondays, be on committees or attend meetings. He also didn't want to be in the employment of the university and beholding to them. We managed that for four years until HR said he had to be an employee due to employment law. Ultimately, it was when he declined a directorship at the university that he became unwanted there. Elfyn had also grown tired of upper management and refused to play ball with them. Both were marked men at the university.'

'It's incredible that the university would be so ruthless with their staff. How did Bear and Elfyn react to being suspended?' asked Parrish.

'The mental and physical health of both men immediately started to decline quite drastically. Elfyn understood what was playing out politically. Bear couldn't or wouldn't accept what was happening. It took an employment law solicitor to tell him that this was the most obvious case of constructive dismissal that she had seen before he accepted what was going on.'

Parrish thought for a moment then said, 'I was going to interview them both. I was hoping they might offer insight into the murder and two deaths. Elfyn sounds like he would be able to make a useful contribution to me. It doesn't sound like Bear would be useful, with his rogue attitude to organisations.'

'My apologies, I haven't explained things very well. Elfyn might indeed be very useful to you. But, as I understand it, he doesn't waste time thinking about the university these days. Bear I'm sure would help and he'd be particularly useful to you.'

'Why do you say that?'

'He sees the world in a different way to many people and he sometimes has an extraordinary insight into people. We meet for lunch every month or two and I know he's been thinking about the case. I'd say he'd have made quite the detective had he chosen to take up such a profession.'

'I look forward to meeting both him and Elfyn soon, if that would be possible?'

'I'll ring them, see what I can arrange. Would you want me to join you?'

'No thanks, but I appreciate the offer. A third person changes the dynamics and focus of such a discussion, sometimes to the detriment, particularly when they know the interviewee. Sorry, bad choice of word.'

'How soon would you like to meet them?'

'As soon as it's convenient to them, and I would like to meet them at home, work, or wherever, but not at the police HQ. The meetings will have to be on different days, it would be too energy sapping for me to do both in the same day.'

'What time is it?' Robbie asked as he looked towards a clock on the wall, before answering his own question, 'just after 8 pm. I'll ring them now.'

Chapter 18 – Furious

It was Friday morning and Robbie had made arrangements for Parrish to visit Elfyn at his work during his lunch break. Before then, Parrish needed to talk to DI Morter and make arrangements for the following week.

Mick, I'm free for a chat whenever you are. P

The text from Parrish resulted less than a minute later with the first few bars of 'Ring of Fire'.

'Good morning, Mick.'

'Morning, Mr P. I have news.'

'Good or bad?'

'Mixed. The best news is that you were spot on with the rainbow lanyard. We got a match with the fibres in the wound on Charlee Butcher's neck.'

'That's great news.'

'The less good news is that DCI Alexanderson asked me to put a note on file of your concerns about a potential threat to the life of Professor Vince Cook. Other than that, no further action without a more credible threat on his life, although I will interview him today. Would you like to join us?'

'Unfortunately, I won't be able to. I'm going to meet Elfyn Williams this afternoon for a chat. I was hoping he might be able to help.'

'You do know he has an alibi, which we have confirmed and he could not have murdered Charlee Butcher?'

'I do indeed. I'm interested to hear what he has to say about his experiences with her and the university. He was employed there for a long time and held some important posts. He'll likely have a good insight into how the place actually functions rather than how we are told it does.'

'OK, I can see that.'

'Similarly, I'm meeting Bear Lawrence at his home on Saturday afternoon.'

'Now that is more like it. We still haven't been able to rule him out as a suspect.'

'And you won't whilst you refuse to accept the limitations posed upon him by his illnesses.'

'As I understand it, you also have similar health issues. Yet here you are, up in Northumberland miles from Helmsley, helping on this case. Surely, Lawrence could have made the journey from his home to Fallodon Hall, which is about half the distance that you have covered?'

'There are scales of illnesses with these health conditions. Take ME as an example. People are often categorized as mild, moderate or severe. People with a mild condition can still work or study or do whatever it is they do, with appropriate changes to accommodate their illness. Using the word 'moderate' to describe ME is perhaps the most inappropriate use of the word in the world. Nevertheless, moderate means you probably can't work, study, or whatever. It is a debilitating illness. Those unfortunate individuals who have a severe case of the condition are bed-bound. Some even need tube-feeding. It's horrendous for them.

'Let me ask you this. When you looked into the possibility that Bear did it, did you find any CCTV, ANPR, mobile phone traces, digital evidence of any kind, that he had left his home and been up in Northumberland near Embleton when Butcher was murdered?'

'No, we did not.'

'What is he then, a magician?'

'He could have used a burner phone, cash, borrowed a car, used false plates or had an accomplice.'

'Really? You believe that?'

'Honestly, no I don't. But we can't rule him out either.'

Silence briefly descended between the two men. Parrish was furious and trying to hold his temper. Not at Bear being a suspect, but at the ignorance towards ME and other chronic illnesses and hidden disabilities. 'Let me ask you this, how many times have you seen me this week?'

'Twice.'

'That's right. Once on Monday for a couple of hours, then briefly on Tuesday afternoon, when I was exhausted and needed to go to bed. Do you know what I have done since then?'

'A lot of thinking about the case?'

'I've been in bed recovering from my efforts at the start of the week and it is now Friday. I know what it is like to live with ME and hopefully you are beginning to understand too.'

Silence descended again. Eventually, DI Morter broke it to confirm he would interview Professor Vince Cook later that day. He wished DCI Parrish good luck with his meetings and said he looked forward to speaking again soon with their findings. Parrish said as little as possible before ending the call with an 'OK'.

Chapter 19 - Whistleblowing

The ride to Belsay on the Honda was sublime through rolling hills doused in golden sunshine. *Northumberland at its finest,* thought Parrish, before adding a caveat, *inland Northumberland at its finest as the coastline was truly staggering too.* The ride noticeably improved his mood after the earlier disagreement with DI Morter.

As he slowed into the entrance that led to the hall, he made a determined effort to concentrate. Elfyn had given directions to follow via his conversation with Robbie when the meeting was arranged. Parrish was stopped at the gate by an English Heritage guide. After a brief exchange, the guide pointed him towards the staff parking area to the left.

Once at the parking, he spotted the red Honda CG125 motorbike belonging to Elfyn outside the old ticket office. He parked his much larger scooter alongside and secured it to the same fence the red motorbike was already using. After locking his helmet and jacket away, he put on a cap and some sunglasses. As he did, he heard the sound of footsteps on the gravel of the carpark. When he turned round, he instantly knew it was Elfyn from the brief description Robbie had given.

Taller than average, with an upright posture that made the most of his height, it was the ginger beard that confirmed his identity. Elfyn didn't stand straight to make the most of his height, it was his usual posture. He was a natural leader, his stance and quiet demeanour instantly brought respect from staff, which he reciprocated.

The two men shook hands and exchanged pleasantries. Elfyn then led them both to a nearby bench in a quiet area of the grounds shaded by trees with an impressive view and the smell of pine hanging in the air. They sat down and Parrish began his gentle questioning. 'Thank you for meeting with me today Elfyn, particularly as it's during your lunch break.'

'Not a problem at all. Robbie tells me that you have been friends for many years. That's good enough for me. I hold him and his opinions in the highest esteem.'

'Thank you, that's very kind of you. Did Robbie tell you that I have ME and fibromyalgia?'

'No, he didn't. I've had ME myself after being ill with Epstein-Barr virus. Fortunately, I recovered after about a year.'

'I hope you don't mind me recording our conversation on my phone then? My memory isn't reliable.'

'Not at all, pleased to be of any help I can.'

'Perhaps we could start off with a bit of background about your time at Embleton University?'

'Of course. I worked with Bear at the university for several years. For a long time, it was a great place to work and we did many good things to improve the student experience, turning them into the professional engineers of tomorrow.

'But then came a creeping disease which eventually swept through the entire university. It involved the woke culture and the #MeToo movement, plus the university began to be run as a money-making machine. This resulted in many below par students being accepted onto courses. The priority was to make loads of money under Napoleon's regime or face staff redundancies to cut costs. This is on record. I've got a copy and I believe Bear has too. I take it you are familiar with who Napoleon is?'

Parrish nodded without saying a word. He didn't want to interrupt this seemingly honest and brutal account.

'Enthusiastic and uneducated staff in HR were brought in and began to infiltrate university life. Silly nonsense from woke culture began to creep in. There was an insidious removal of experienced administration staff in HR, replaced by business partners with no experience of either business or how the university worked.

'It wasn't restricted to HR. They cut our funding. Their policy seemed to be to get rid of all teaching staff and to keep research staff only. 'Research pays' was their mantra. But it doesn't, money comes from teaching, from student fees. They were too stupid to realise that. Research brings in grants to fund very specific research described in a grant. It is effectively spent once the grant is awarded and it does nothing to swell the coffers of the university.

'Self-centred morons came into management, followed by their yes-men to seemingly back them up. Lots of very good engineers were lost before I left and even a few afterwards. Sycophants replaced good engineers. Despite this, it was still a half decent university albeit with a woke brigade. Although they were starting to see the fallout with poor graduates not fit for the workplace and poor feedback from the same.

'The whole set up seemed to be aimed at getting rid of middle-aged men. Engineers like Bear and I are more expensive to employ than lecturers wet behind the ears. It was all about cost-cutting. People without scruples were happy to facilitate it. It left academics worried for their future, for their careers. Most were too frightened to put their heads above the parapet and call out this behaviour and regime, unlike Bear and myself. There was an insidious nastiness, which led to rot, and rot stinks.

'The knives were out for us, by our not contributing to research. That was also nonsense. Bear was employed on a teaching contract but was an active researcher and prolific publisher of peer-reviewed scientific papers. It's worth mentioning that he published twice at the Embleton Teaching Conference in the months before we were both suspended. He wrote both pieces with contributions from the rest of us on The Design and Manufacture module. Consequently, he was lead author and we were all named as authors too, which was generous of him. What is important is that he used these publications to document the huge increase in student numbers with the same staffing and the consequent decline in educational standards. Management wasn't listening to us, so Bear thought publishing hard facts might get through to them. I don't know if the management saw these but if they did, they wouldn't have been happy.

'I had been Director of Teaching and helped create two project modules and one other module. I was initially module leader on all three of them and later Bear was. The project modules were difficult to manage and they cost money to operate because the student's manufactured and tested their designs. The school management wanted these modules replaced with book exercises, which are much cheaper to run. The result of this are graduates with less experience, fewer practical skills and a lack of innovative approach to engineering solutions.

'There is an irony to all this. It's rumour, but one I have heard too many times. Napoleon was allegedly accused of sexual harassment. Female staff were refusing to be in a room alone with him. Eager young women were more inclined to do what he wanted with the promise of promotion, older women were more fearful. Female staff started leaving. He was dodgy and dangerous. The cull of staff at his direction was likely done in part to deflect attention from his behaviour. Bear and I fitted the bill. Teachers by contract, not by research, we taught expensive modules and were paid more than junior staff. Off for the chop!'

Elfyn stopped his rant, seemingly to draw breath. When Parrish considered that he would get no more without another question, he asked one after some thought. Robbie had said Elfyn often saw the bigger picture and he framed his question to suit, despite it being a longer question than he would normally ask.

'Natasha Horseman. Presumably you know she is dead now, suicide apparently. Did you know her? Would someone hold a grudge against her sufficiently to murder her? What are your thoughts?'

'Only met her once or twice. She was at the suspension meeting. She said little and knew even less. The letters I received from her afterwards said little too. She was ineffectual, but why would anyone murder her? She hurt me and was similarly worse towards others. Perhaps someone might hold a grudge, but murder? I doubt it. I'm familiar with the area where she died. The cliffs are dangerous, especially when it is windy. It is utterly plausible that she fell to her death, others have also committed suicide there.'

Again, Elfyn stopped having seemingly said as much as he felt necessary about Natasha Horseman.

'Same question about Dr Carlang,' asked Parrish.

'Largely ineffectual, failed academic. No fire or interest. Fell into various roles because he wasn't very good at anything. Sat on committees, sometimes chaired them. Committees that were tick-box exercises. With my role as Director of Teaching, I was often on some of these committees. It was utterly infuriating that I couldn't be effective with such a spineless chair as Carlang. He was careless, inadequate, highly-influenced, he sucked-up and offered no fairness to the people he was instructed to beat on. He wrote a grossly inaccurate and biased report about Bear and I, even before interviewing the students, which is on record. It was a done deal.

'CB was telling Napoleon to get rid of us. Suspension was used as an act of aggression. She was instrumental to all of this. She sat in on meetings with Carlang, was obnoxious and with no understanding was asking questions about teaching. The minutes from the meetings, which she took, were wholly inaccurate. I returned my heavily revised version of them, which went largely ignored. They were operating kangaroo courts and spineless Carlang did their bidding.'

'You've already mentioned CB, which I take to be Charlee Butcher. How well did you know her?'

'Met her only once but had numerous emails and letters from her.'

'What did you think of her?'

'Anyone who met her would immediately know that she was the most unpleasant person in the world.' He paused briefly. 'No, that's unfair. It would take maybe five seconds to come to that conclusion. I ask myself, 'what was CB's relationship with Napoleon?' who disappeared soon after we did. Why was that? He should have been suspended for what he had done. But he was too influential to be suspended and investigated. In all likelihood, he jumped before he was pushed and is probably ruining another institution as we speak. He showed nastiness of forethought, manipulation of staff and students. He encouraged students to throw dirt at us which was unsubstantiated. If any harm had befallen to any of the students, well, no tears from me.'

'Who do you think murdered Charlee Butcher?'

'Don't know and I'm not surprised she was murdered. Nasty piece of work. I pay more attention to dirt on the street than people in my past who have harmed me.'

'Was the death of Carlang suspicious to you?

'He was a turd. Ineffectual. Did the dirty on behalf of others. Did it merit murder? Probably not.'

'Who should worry that they might be next?'

'Don't know. Napoleon or the Pro V-C possibly? They were a clique, likeminded egotists. Lots of unpleasant people who slithered out of the woodwork, they were scared of their shadows. Half of HR should be worried. The two halves of HR hated each other. They all had it in for each other. Stabbing in the back was common and on record if you knew which documents to look at. In the frame for murder? About twenty people were forced out by the nest of vipers around CB and Napoleon. Of the ten most obnoxious people I had dealings with at the university, three are now dead.'

'That's incredibly insightful and useful to me, thank you. Before we wind this up, is there anything else that you would like to tell me?'

'In a word, whistleblowing. Irrespective of the murders, which may be unfortunate without link or coincidence, the number of people injured by the activities of these people should result in whistleblowing, which I would be happy to initiate.

Whistleblowers, please get in touch!' he pretended to shout.

'Legally, time on whistleblowing is not limited, so once the woke brigade leave, decency will prevail and these people may be held to account. Murder is a step too far, but not a sound slaughtering in the courts, which is entirely appropriate. Some justice might even prevail, five, ten, fifteen or even twenty years from now. They might even be at another university or place of work, but they will get their comeuppance. Mark my words.'

Chapter 20 – email
scratcher010980@yahoo.com

The following morning, Parrish enjoyed breakfast with his hosts as they sat at the dining table. Robbie asked how the meeting had gone with Elfyn. Parrish confirmed it was useful in his understandings of both the case and how the university went about its business.

In turn, he asked both his hosts about their plans for the weekend. They didn't need to ask him what he was doing. They merely wished him well with his meeting with Bear Lawrence and looked forward to him returning on Monday after a short break back in his cottage in Helmsley.

The ride south from Embleton was enjoyable, if not quite as good as the ride to Belsay Hall the previous day. Too much motorway and not enough scenery. The last few miles from the main roads, which led to Bear's cottage were more to Parrish's liking, countryside and fields of green, yellow and gold.

Bear had texted Parrish instructions to find the cottage as he claimed it was difficult to find. Parrish had ignored the warning and put the postcode for Bear's address into his satnav. It brought him to a pub carpark in the village, which was surrounded by old cottages and a mixture of houses from different periods.

He dug out his phone and read the text to the end this time. He still rode straight past the cottage and had to turn after the post office, just as Bear had warned,

If you've got to the post office, you've gone too far and you'll have to turn around.

Having turned around, the instructions to find the cottage made perfect sense and it was only seconds later when he pulled onto the off-street parking on Bear's property. With nothing obviously secure to lock the Honda to, he settled on fitting a disk lock on the front wheel and his chain through the rear wheel.

As he crunched across the gravel to the picket-fence gate leading to Bear's garden, he was hit by a floral assault of honeysuckle and clematis. These and other plants climbed a trellis to make a wall dividing the garden from the parking area, providing colour, scent and privacy. The welcoming flowers and aroma contrasted with the furious barking of a small terrier in the garden. Consequently, Parrish made a cautious approach to opening the gate which led to the garden.

Bear was relaxing on a rattan chair in a patio area in front of the house. He was dressed in shorts and t-shirt, wearing shades and a wide-brimmed sun hat.

He had heard the scooter and gave a wave when he saw Parrish, shouting 'come on through, she's friendly'.

The ferocity of the little terrier's barking was not reassuring and Parrish cautiously entered the garden. Once inside, the little dog put her front paws on his leg, gave one last bark, before turning to run back down the garden path to Bear. Her tail was wagging as she skipped along, clearly proud of herself.

'Is he alright, he looks like he has a limp?'

'She's Rosie and that is a terrier skip. Please take a seat,' smiled Bear.

'Lovely village and nice place you have here,' said Parrish as he sat down in another rattan chair in front of the house.

'Is that a Honda Forza?'

'It is, a 350.'

'Very nice. I've got a Piaggio Beverly 300.'

The two men chatted about motorbikes and scooters for a short time. However, it was almost uncomfortably hot sat in front of the white cottage despite them being in Northern England. Bear saw that it might be a bit too warm for his guest who was wearing motorbike jeans and boots. 'Proper little sun trap this is. Would you prefer to sit inside, it's much cooler in there?'

'If you don't mind, plus we can talk in private.'

Bear opened one half of the patio doors, which led inside his home. Rosie bounded in first over the step, Bear held the door open for his guest to enter then followed on behind.

From outside, the interior of the house appeared almost black, a trick of the light. Once inside, Parrish was surprised by the well-lit room. He also lived in a two-bedroom cottage, with a living room and a separate kitchen/diner downstairs and was expecting similar. The wall between the two downstairs rooms had been removed here to make a long living room with a dining table at one end. Two doors led off to other rooms. *A kitchen and maybe a porch, utility room or bathroom,* thought Parrish for the other.

As with his cottage, stairs ran up to the floor above. Also like his cottage, there was a black wood burner. There was one other similarity. Both Bear and himself must like Chesterfields, but the seating here was very different to his recliner and two-seater settee. Sat along one wall was the longest settee he had ever seen. It was in a Chesterfield style and sported a light-coloured brown leather. 'That's quite the settee,' remarked Parrish.

'Please take a seat. We had it made to suit our needs. Long enough that Liz and I can both stretch out and still have enough space for Rosie. I spend an inordinate amount of time laid on the sofa.'

'The case notes revealed that you have ME and fibromyalgia. I don't know whether you know, but I have the same?'

'I didn't know. You have my sympathies. It's a curse to have these and other chronic illnesses. But as ever, I always try to look on the bright side. Perhaps you will be the first policeman to believe my alibi or do I remain a suspect?'

Parrish looked down, briefly ashamed of his colleague's attitudes towards Bear's illnesses. 'I won't lie to you, you will remain a suspect until we either find the killer, or have absolute proof that you couldn't have murdered Charlee Butcher. Having said that, I believe that you are innocent.'

'Why is that? We've neither met nor spoken before today.'

'I'm both a detective and a person living with chronic illnesses. Please don't be offended by my observations. Your arms lack bulk as a result of muscle atrophy. I doubt that you would be strong enough to have attacked, carried and murdered the victim. The only rattan chair outside with a cushioned seat was the one you were sat on. There is a blanket on one end of the settee here, where presumably you sit. Whilst the blanket could be to keep warm in the cooler months, it maybe that without a cushion of some sort, you find sitting uncomfortable because your gluteus maximus is not what it was due to your sedentary lifestyle.'

'Very good. Yes, my bottom isn't as big as it used to be, something I can't say for my belly,' laughed Bear, 'can I get you a drink?'

'Water would be fine.'

At that Bear disappeared through the far door, which Parrish now presumed led to the kitchen. When Bear reappeared, carrying glasses of chilled water for them both, Parrish's eyes had readjusted to the indoor lighting. For the first time he saw Bear clearly without a hat and sunglasses. Short, cropped, salt and pepper hair sat above big blue eyes and long black eyelashes. Like Parrish, he too wore a stubble beard and probably because he also lacked the energy and desire to be clean shaven every day. The absence of a watch and no tan line brought Parrish's approval.

Both men also seemingly had the same approach to discussions. They preferred to remain silent and let others speak whilst they listened. When neither spoke, Bear broke the impasse out of politeness. 'So, where do we start?' Which was his attempt to make Parrish do the talking. 15-love to Bear.

'How about you talk about Charlee Butcher?' 15 all.

'The one whose name we don't use?' laughed Bear. Parrish looked at him quizzically.

'Elfyn and I used to call her that in our telephone conversations. It was partly a nod to Voldemort, the archenemy of Harry Potter and partly because I found it difficult to talk about her, even to say her name. Just to be clear, whatever I say today is from my perspective only. If you want to know how Elfyn feels, you should ask him yourself.'

'I did, yesterday, and he would only call her CB.'

'She was involved from start to finish in having me suspended and then dismissed from Embleton University, and then through all the Employment Tribunal process. She even arranged for a very sizeable payment to be made to me to keep it out of the courts by my closing the tribunal case and signing a non-disclosure agreement. To me, that payment is an admittance of guilt on behalf of the university for the unjust and abhorrent treatment that I suffered at their hands.

'At no point did she allow me fair treatment. She frequently lied and misrepresented information. The consequences of her actions were to end both my careers as a researcher and as a lecturer. I've lost my income and can no longer add to my pension as I had planned to for my retirement. Worse, she caused my health to be irrecoverably damaged, at least with medical knowledge as it stands today. Diagnoses of my illnesses through medical tests are at best years away and there are no treatments, let alone cures, on the horizon either.

'I've definitely got motive to murder her and I'll admit to entertaining involuntary thoughts of doing so. Would I do it, did I do it? No.'

'Fair points, well made. There isn't much I can say about that having previously spoken to both Robbie and Elfyn. Anything else that you would like to add?'

'This may sound odd, but I truly believe she was in league with the devil. We sat opposite each other for about an hour, the only time I ever met her, and I could not have told you what she looked like afterwards. Since then, her face has been in the media and I now know what she looks like. Very rarely have I truly felt the force of evil in my presence, but I did that day.'

Parrish was mindful of what Robbie had said to him about Bear's insight. 'That's very interesting. I'm a keen listener if you have any more that you would like to share with me?'

'I'm not a psychologist, but I have my own thoughts and feelings about the killer. I'm fairly sure that I haven't met them, but I have met the victim. Victim being the wrong word in my opinion for The Butcher. The killer feels compelled to do this, it's almost involuntarily but they're not a schizophrenic. It's not obsession and it's not about money, sex or any other normal driver to murder. It's about justice, right and wrong, good versus evil, you might say.'

'That's fascinating, thank you. Let's return to your experiences with the university. Hypothetically speaking of course, why do you think the university chose to force you out?'

'Because I speak my mind and act according to my values.'

'Can you give me examples?'

'My utmost priority was the education and welfare of the students, closely followed by the same for staff. Making money for the university was some way down my list of priorities. Their determination to cut staff numbers and increase student numbers was obscene. Then there was the fiasco of introducing a new degree that none of the staff wanted. When they asked me to be a director for the new degree, I politely declined. That was the point at which I became persona non grata and my fate was sealed. They simply took the first opportunity they could to get rid of me, which were complaints initially about a colleague. They pushed him under the bus first then pushed me too.'

'Thank you, Bear. Robbie had told me the bones of this and you are filling it all in. What can you tell me about Dr Carlang?'

'Only met him the once too. Spineless, weak individual, trying desperately to curry faith with management by doing their dirty work for them. I expect they despised the disgusting individual that he was, almost as much as I did.'

'What did he do to make you feel this way?'

'He wrote a report, no doubt orchestrated by The Butcher, which manipulated, misled, and quite simply ignored the truth. When he presented this at the final meeting he lied even more and added fuel to the fire.

'Do you know that he claimed that the students had credibility because some provided dates for when the allegations allegedly happened? One date for an allegation against me was given as the final day of the first term. That could not be true because it wasn't a teaching slot in the timetable. It was for submission of documents to Robbie for marking. Whether she was told of this error, or realised it herself afterwards, I know not. What I do know is that she amended the date to over one month earlier. This also had to be untrue because it was a Wednesday and I only taught on this module on a Friday.

'Another student submitted a screenshot of a text she sent referring to another allegation. That allegation was in reference to Elfyn and not me. Separately, I asked the investigation to look into attendance of both the students and staff. This was never done. For the date provided on the screenshot, I was on sick leave with a back injury. This was known to several staff involved in the investigation, but nobody mentioned it. I only found out about these dates after the investigation was complete and the report written. So not only was this allegation nothing to do with me, I wasn't even on campus at the alleged time. Yet it was taken as proof of the credibility of the students, whilst my credibility was never considered. Look, I could go on, but what would it prove?'

'I've known Robbie Mustoe since school days. He has told me that both you and Elfyn are honest, upstanding individuals with sound morals. Your impassioned words absolutely confirm that. Let me ask you now the same for Professor Vince Cook?'

'Never met the man. When I was going through all this at the university, I could neither face reading their emails or letters nor was I able to do so. I forwarded communications to Robbie who would summarize them in a few sentences so that I had a grasp of what was going on. I was in no fit state to engage with the university and its corrupt processes.

'Months later when I was a little better, I was able to read a transcript of the meeting PVC proceeded over and a letter giving his decision from the meeting. A meeting which took place in my absence, whilst I was on sick leave. Even in the transcript he reveals his bias against me, several times. He asked if I showed any reconciliation towards the students? Why would I? They were making fictional allegations against me on dates that proved I was not present. He deserves a similar fate to Butcher and Carlang.'

'Perhaps you should keep that opinion to yourself. Besides, Carlang's death isn't considered suspicious to the police.'

'Well, it is to me. Someone probably turned his machine off, stood on a breathing tube or poisoned the bugger and got away with it.'

Parrish stayed tight-lipped on this as he held exactly the same thoughts. 'When Robbie described you to me, he paid you many compliments.'

'Well, that was very kind of him.'

'He said that if you had turned your mind to it, you would have made an excellent detective.'

'I will thank him for the compliment when I next speak to him, but he's wrong.'

'How so?'

'I'm a sensitive soul and an empath. I have nightmares after watching a crime drama on TV late at night. No way could I cope with seeing a real murder scene,' laughed Bear.

Parrish grinned then turned serious. 'Look Bear, there is a killer out there that I want to catch. I am not so proud that I will ignore the help of an amateur sleuth. Can you help me with the investigation and to catch the killer with your insight?'

'That's not a question or offer that I expected. But, as it happens, something did come to mind.'

Parrish leant towards Bear involuntarily. 'This sounds interesting, go on.'

'Well, I've been following the case as best I could via the media and something struck me. It was when I was watching the reconstruction of her last jog from her house that appeared on Crime Scene. The piece mentioned that the reconstruction was based on CCTV, digital data and eye-witness reports.'

'That's true.'

'Do you know that I was a Commercial Helicopter Pilot and Flight Instructor?'

'I do indeed. Most impressive.'

Bear ignored the compliment. 'Over the years, I must have flown over Northumberland hundreds, if not thousands, of times. The murder was committed near Fallodon Hall, which itself is near Brunton Airfield. I know this because Fallodon Hall is just to the left of an approach to Brunton Airfield. Brunton Airfield was an RAF base, but has been shut for years. The three runways remain and you're not allowed to use them without permission of the Air Ministry. But that doesn't prevent aircraft from making approaches to the runways in training exercises, which is frequently done, as indeed I have. Do you know if the investigation has considered who might have been flying in the vicinity when the murder was committed?'

'To the best of my knowledge, this hasn't been looked at. But why would it be relevant, a pilot would be looking at the runway, not the woods below him?'

'Another nearby airfield is Eshott, a place that I've flown over and in and out of, many times. Eshott and the like aren't large or international airports with medium or heavy aircraft taking passengers to destinations all around the world. They're small airfields where private pilots and some commercial pilots fly in and out of, mostly over the local area. They fly in small aircraft, mainly microlights, fixed wing and light helicopters.'

'I'm still not with you on this.'

'Almost all of these flights are made for the pleasure of flying, hour building or training. Pilots and passengers often make video recordings of their flights. It struck me that someone may have potentially filmed Butcher on her run or even being murdered.'

'But that would take an age to follow up with all the flights and hours and hours of footage to examine. We're at the back end of the investigation and resources are tight.'

'No, it wouldn't. Contact the clubs at these airfields. They'll have records of who flew when and where. It was a Monday evening in the Spring. Not many aircraft will have been flying. You only need one flight in the vicinity with a video recording to maybe help you catch the killer.'

'That's a really good idea. Could you give me a list of airfields, clubs, or anything the investigation needs to look into?

'Of course, what's your email address?'

'scratcher010980@yahoo.com'

Chapter 21 – Some thoughts of mine

It had been late Saturday afternoon when Parrish parked his Forza in his garage in Helmsley. After taking calories and fluids on-board, together with the final medications for the day, he went to bed early. As soon as his head hit the soft down pillow, he fell asleep.

Waking to the usual fatigue, he was pleased to find he was in discomfort rather than pain. He decided to make himself a hearty breakfast and was looking forward to it as he descended the stairs in his cottage. Within seconds of looking in the fridge, he was reminded that he had been away for a week. There was very little in the fridge as he had binned anything that would have gone off whilst he was away.

Time for Plan B. It was still early and the hordes of visitors to Helmsley would not have arrived in their droves yet. The roads, marketplace and Co-op would still be quiet. It was thirty minutes since he had taken his lansoprazole. He had thirty more to walk to the supermarket and back to buy some food, cook it and eat it before taking his next lot of medication.

Feeling suitably sated with his breakfast, he decided to help his digestion with a black coffee. *Forgot to check if I had any pods left,* he thought to himself. If he didn't have any, he wasn't prepared to wade through the possibly now busy town centre to buy some. Fortunately, a couple of pods were still in his cupboard and he enjoyed a coffee relaxing on his Chesterfield recliner.

The Chesterfield made his mind drift to meeting Bear the previous afternoon and sitting on his Chesterfield. *Looking for aviation footage was a good shout. We're so use to our own drone recordings, we forget who else is flying. After coffee, I'll check my emails for one from Bear about airfields. I'll forward it to Mick with a written update on progress.*

Parrish revised his plan for the day. Instead of checking emails first, he put his used laundry from the last week in the washing machine. Then he repacked for the forthcoming week up in Embleton. This included making up the little plastic pots of the daily medication that he took at breakfast. He also had to ensure that he had enough of the lansoprazole and naproxen that he took at other times of the day.

Back on the Chesterfield, he fired up the laptop he had on loan. In his inbox he found an email from Bear. Within it was a short list of airfields, aero clubs and contacts. These he forwarded to DI Morter together with a narrative explaining Bear's suggestion.

The next task would take much longer. When he was still working for the Metropolitan Police, younger colleagues had suggested he used technology to turn audio recordings into written text. Whilst that would work, technology can't capture the nuances of the interviewee's responses like the human ear can. Parrish took a pride in his reading of people and preferred the old-fashioned way, with just a nod to new technology.

In years gone by he'd have used pen and paper. Now he opened a new document in word and prepared to make notes as he listened to the recording of the interview with Dr Elfyn Williams. He typed occasional words and phrases as he listened, but he wasn't quite fast enough and kept having to stop the recording. When he had played it through once, he repeated the exercise, knowing that with his poor concentration and inconsistent memory he may have missed some key points.

Happy that he had captured the salient points of the interview, he read through them several times. He thought about what he already knew from conversations with Robbie, DI Morter, Bear and interview notes he had read on the database. Now, he slowly started to type his thoughts down into sentences and paragraphs. He used question marks and bold to help him develop his thoughts. It read as follows:

What is clear is that Embleton was once a harmonious institution with a focus on not just good education, but on producing the professional engineers of tomorrow. Now it is in turmoil, focused on making money, unhappy students and sub-standard graduates were the result. There had been a sea change. It is unclear where this had started exactly. The Personnel Department had become HR and a new Director appointed, **Heledd Morgan. Could she be a suspect, a target or both? Does she have an alibi? MM will know from the investigation.**

She had brought in new, young, inexperienced staff and got rid of experienced staff. HR was potentially split in two halves, not as an organisation, but by experience, values, business attitudes. **New business managers were appointed. Who had applied but not got appointed? Ask Rachel Sturridge about the culture of HR and possibly being in two halves. (Important because of rainbow lanyard being the murder weapon, could be someone from HR).**

Woke culture, the #MeToo movement had apparently spread through the university. Elfyn had considered this bad, but clearly not everyone at the university held the same opinion. **Was the university split in two, like HR? Traditionalists** versus modernists? Did this matter sufficiently to make someone kill? (Probably not).

Bear and Elfyn had spoken out, published even about declining standards. They had been forced out of the university. They had been potential suspects, but others had also been forced out. **Check list from Heledd Morgan with MM.**

Could the 'three little piggies' be four, five or more? Napoleon could be a target but was also a very real suspect as he had left the university. **Where was Napoleon now and does he have an alibi? Who else might be a piggy?**

Could the killer be someone he had sexually harassed (allegedly) who was angered that he had escaped justice? Anger aimed at Napoleon and the three little piggies? (Good line of enquiry).

Carlang was a yes-man. Part of the kangaroo courts. So was the Pro V-C. Carlang was dead, so was Butcher. **Surely, PVC was a possible victim. What reason would he have to murder his colleagues?**

Whistleblowing. Lots of staff had gone from HR and the university. In particular, experienced administration staff and lecturers. **Had the investigation already looked at staff who had left since the Personnel Department became HR?**

Perhaps Natasha Horseman's death was suicide? Was her death skewing my investigation? Maybe accept it was a suicide? (I'm not convinced myself but might help to gain focus).

Parrish lent back in the Chesterfield. His battery was nearly spent. To prevent wasting any more energy, he decided to email it as it was to DI Morter with the title:

Some thoughts of mine

Chapter 22 – It's a deal

For what was left of Sunday, Parrish mostly relaxed at home in the cottage and tried to forget the case. He did have to finish packing and put the freshly washed clothes in the tumble dryer. As a treat, he picked up a Chinese takeaway and washed it down with a chilled Pinot Grigio. With a belly full of food and a glass of wine inside of him, he fell asleep in his favourite chair. Match of the Day 2 was playing on the TV when he awoke close to 11 pm, so he turned the TV off and dragged his aching body up to bed.

The following morning, he could afford to take his time getting ready before the two-hour ride to the police HQ at Embleton. DI Morter had agreed to meet him at 2 pm. Parrish planned to go straight to Robbie's home and his temporary accommodation, once the meeting with DI Morter was finished.

* * *

'Good to see you Mr P. How was Helmsley?'

'Good to see you, and Helmsley was good too. Nice to get a couple of nights in my own bed. I love staying with Robbie and Christine, plus they have such a lovely home, but there is nothing like your own bed, is there?'

DI Morter nodded in agreement. Parrish suddenly realised he knew nothing of Mick's private life. He might have all sorts going on in the background. Life can be very challenging at times. Normally, Parrish would have asked Mick how his weekend was, but decided to move on to business. 'Apologies for sending you my rough notes and not something more polished and appropriate.'

'No need to apologise at all. They were fascinating to read and I spent much of Sunday addressing them. Plenty to do still, but should we talk through them?'

'By all means.'

The next hour was spent discussing Parrish's notes and what DI Morter could tell him from the investigation to date, including the interview with PVC. DI Morter had already pre-typed responses and suggested actions to follow up where necessary to help the discussion and to prioritise their next moves. Together they agreed to interview Heledd Morgan the following day. Whether it would just be DI Morter interviewing, or also Parrish, was undecided. It would depend on whether Parrish felt he had enough energy to attend.

Heledd Morgan had an alibi for the murder of Charlee Butcher, but she still had a lot of questions to answer. Some of these they would email her today ahead of the interview. They needed to know who had been appointed to positions of business manager during her tenure. More importantly, they needed to know who had applied for these posts but been unsuccessful. Such people may have motive and could be suspects for the murder of Charlee Butcher.

Morgan would be asked in the interview, in the strongest terms, if necessary, about her department, HR, and the wider university. Was there a division within HR of new staff versus longer serving, more experienced staff? Did a similar divide exist within the university, possibly a traditionalist versus modernist split? Those who wanted the university to continue as it had for eons and those who favoured money-making over educational values.

They were also keen to learn in more detail about the day-to-day running of HR. Heledd had previously described the hierarchy of HR, with the business managers dealing with day-to-day operations. Who really wielded power over most of the HR staff? Was it Heledd Morgan or the business managers? With Charlee Butcher having an important and slightly different role to the other business managers who looked after faculty matters, did she hold power?

Heledd would also be getting a grilling about the allegations of sexual harassment of female staff by Napoleon. DI Morter and Parrish expected that she would deny that any allegations were made. In a phone call from Parrish to Elfyn Williams after his interview, Elfyn had revealed some names of women linked to the allegations. If Heledd Morgan did deny the allegations, they would reveal some of the names supplied by Elfyn and suggest the interview be terminated so those women could be interviewed. They hoped this would then likely cause her to now discuss the allegations and the course of action or otherwise against Napoleon.

Following the interview with Heledd Morgan, Rachel Sturridge would be interviewed, which Parrish would both attend and lead. He had met her previously, whereas DI Morter hadn't. Parrish felt he understood how to frame the questions best to get information out of her. She would also be asked about the divide in HR and the university.

As well as these two interviews planned for the following day, there were several lines of enquiry that had been covered and some to follow up. All of these, DI Morter and other detectives assigned temporarily back on the case, would investigate.

But there was an elephant in the room. It was the death of Natasha Horseman, was it suicide or murder? Eventually, it was DI Morter who mentioned it. 'I think you are right to accept that the death of Natasha Horseman was suicide.'

'It may help us focus on the murder of Charlee Butcher at the moment. But I would like to look into the deaths of both Horseman and Carlang. Perhaps you could arrange authorisation so that I might access the information stored on those as well as the Butcher murder?' asked Parrish in as pleasant a manner as he could muster.

A pause ensued caused by DI Morter breathing out loudly. 'I'm under orders to accept the conclusions of those deaths as they are and not to investigate them any further. The powers that be are impressed, extremely pleased and very grateful for you identifying the type of murder weapon, as indeed am I. The suggestion is that we turn your impressive insight to finding Charlee Butcher's missing phone.'

Now it was Parrish's turn to pause the discussion. He looked down, picked up a pen and tapped it on the desk whilst he thought. 'I'll do a deal with you. If I help you find the phone, or we find good reason for us to look into those deaths, then you give me access to all the information I've asked for.'

'It's a deal.'

They shook hands. Parrish felt certain that somehow or other, be it finding the phone or otherwise, he'd eventually get the extra database access he wanted.

Chapter 23 – Forced to stop

After the meeting, Parrish rode back to Robbie and Christine's place. With the Honda stowed in the garage, he detached the large top box from the rear of the scooter. Within it were the clothes, toiletries, medication, etc. that he needed for the next week.

With the top box and contents deposited in the guest bedroom, Parrish headed for the living room and levered open his loaned laptop. Whilst it fired up annoyingly slowly to Parrish, he started to try and think like the killer. More specifically, he tried to think like the killer immediately after the murder.

The killer had removed Charlee Butcher's phone from the holder on her upper left arm and replaced it with an identical model. Why had the killer done that? He hadn't done it to steal it for financial value, as he had replaced it like for like. He'd stolen it because the contents of the phone had value. That was why, thought Parrish.

But to whom did the contents hold value? Charlee Butcher certainly, but she was now dead. Were the contents of value to the killer? Possibly. But in what way? Did the killer want to read the contents, or did they want to prevent the police from reading the contents? Both interesting possibilities, but without the phone or the killer explaining why, it would remain a mystery.

Killers usually flee the scene of the crime. Where they end up is often predictable. Most go home. Sometimes they go to their parents, particularly mothers. They behave like children and mummy can always put things right, can't she? They also flee to ports such as Dover or Felixstowe and to airports, Heathrow, Gatwick and the like. A few are found as far as they can get on the solid ground of Blighty, Land's End or John o' Groats.

This killer had moved from the murder scene towards Embleton. The investigation had discovered this from Charlee Butcher's phone pinging a mast. This meant the killer was probably either heading for home or his parents. Where were either of these places? mused Parrish.

Finally, the laptop finished doing whatever was necessary to make it useable. Parrish started looking at a map of Northumberland and slowly zoomed in on Embleton as the centre. Other than Embleton, there were no large settlements within a few miles, so that was the most likely place that the killer was heading to. Parrish knew where the murder scene was, close to Fallodon Hall, and he began to consider routes the killer may have taken from there to Embleton.

It was 2.3 miles by road and six minutes by car, estimated Google. Fifty-one minutes by foot too. *Both predictions used almost identical routes via roads. There was no good reason to believe the killer had taken this route and more reasons to rule it out. It was the most direct route and had been thoroughly investigated already with no results.* It seemed more likely to Parrish that the killer was on foot avoiding roads for most of the journey to protect their identity.

Now Parrish turned to looking online at Ordnance Survey maps of the area. *The killer may have headed south east on footpaths mainly through woods towards Christon Bank. This village was effectively divided in half by the main railway line running north and south between Edinburgh and London. There was no railway station in Embleton, so the killer hadn't taken the train.*

The killer may have left a vehicle in one half of Christon Bank and used roads to continue their journey. Unlikely, thought Parrish. *It was an unnecessary complication for such a short journey and the killer was likely fit and strong so travelling by foot was no problem. It was more likely that the killer would have headed east from here on foot towards Embleton.*

The problem with this route was Christon Bank. Albeit a small village, the very real possibility existed of the killer being seen by someone in the village or nearby such as a dog walker, jogger or passing motorist. The investigation had been thorough and there were no suspects or persons of interest having been in the area either before or after the murder within a reasonable timeframe.

So which possible route had the killer taken, thought Parrish as he zoomed out a little on the map? Tracks and footpaths headed north east in the direction of Brunton and Lower Brunton. All of these potential routes crossed the same railway line that passed through Christon Bank to the south. Both Bruntons were tiny, with very few houses. Lower Brunton was effectively one house. *Much less chance of being spotted travelling in this direction than the route via Christon Bank*, thought Parrish. Plus, several footpaths avoided both of the Bruntons entirely. Two footpaths from this area then led back to Embleton over open country side and some woodland.

The killer took one of these routes north east towards the Bruntons, thought Parrish, *but which one?* He considered the options still using the OS maps. All of the options had to cross the railway line, which had only two crossing points in this area, which narrowed the options down. Pertinently, the killer may well have crossed the railway line at these locations before or after the murder. *More lines of enquiry, if you forgive the pun,* chuckled Parrish to himself.

He looked at the database for the search areas. They extended to the railway line and stopped there. A very real physical barrier. It was a busy railway line with high-speed trains. An intrinsic part of the transport network of the UK and it was protected by fences.

Except for 'moveable' barriers at road crossings and the like, realised Parrish. He switched back to Google maps and chose the satellite option. This allowed him to look down on the railway line and follow it over the area he was interested in. There were three crossings that the killer may have used, one at Christon Bank and two more to the north between Fallodon Hall and the Bruntons.

Had the railway crossings been closed for a passing train when the killer had tried to cross? Perhaps CCTV fitted to the train had pictured the killer waiting? wondered Parrish. He could find no evidence on the database that this had been considered. *Put this in an email to Mick later for investigation.*

Frustrated that he had hit a stop, Parrish cursed his poor concentration and his illness for dragging him off track. He was supposed to be finding the phone, thinking like the killer, not simply following the route of the killer. To break his chain of thought, Parrish went to the kitchen for a drink of water.

Sitting back in his chair, the laptop went unwatched on the coffee table. Parrish refocused on finding the phone. *Had the killer kept the phone? Perhaps to take their time to look at the contents carefully? Perhaps as a memento?* questioned Parrish. *If the killer had kept it, the reason might be to take time to look at it, which was plausible. Depending on the content, perhaps it was a memento as a link to the now deceased Charlee Butcher?*

No, the killer hadn't kept the phone, concluded Parrish. *Charlee Butcher was a very private person, careful. Her phone would be protected somehow. Iris recognition or fingerprint were possible, as was a password or making a shape on the screen. The killer wouldn't be able to access the contents. But the police probably could if they got hold of it. The killer had swapped phones. Would he spend time searching through the contents at the murder site? Probably not,* concluded Parrish. *The phone had moved and then stopped pinging masts. That meant one of three things, the battery had gone flat, the phone had been turned off, or the phone had broken.*

Parrish considered these options. *Had the battery gone flat? Unlikely coincidence. Would Butcher have gone running with a phone with next to no charge? Probably not.* He ruled that option out. *Had the killer turned it off? Had the killer smashed it? Both were plausible, arguably the killer would be more likely to attempt to destroy it and the contents with it. Why do either? They took it to look at the contents or to keep as a memento?*

So, they didn't intend to take it and turn it off until it was safe to do so. So, why did they suddenly turn it off? Were they home? Unlikely, it hadn't pinged masts in Embleton and there were few houses in the area. Maybe because they had tried to access the contents and found that they couldn't get in, realised Parrish with satisfaction.

The killer had fled the scene with the intention of looking at the phone later. So why had they stopped in mid-flight to look at it, pondered Parrish? *Curiosity got the better of them? Unlikely.*

Parrish spoke out loud to himself. 'It was because the killer was forced to stop. A railway crossing was closed. They stopped, looked at the phone, couldn't get into it and binned it! Yes!' he shouted and punched the air.

After another drink of water to quench his thirst and calm his excitement down, Parrish rang Mick. DI Morter confirmed that the railway line was taken as the boundary of the search at the north east boundary of the search area. DS Ash had made the decision, which he had endorsed as the railway line had secure fencing in that area, making it unlikely the killer had crossed it. As such, they hadn't searched that section of the railway. Further south, near Christon Bank, some of the railway had been searched with drones but to no avail. With it being the mainline, they were reluctant to request permission to close the line without good reason.

It was agreed that DI Morter would have his team make enquires to the possibility of CCTV footage from trains that had used the tracks around the time of the murder. He would also arrange for a search of track with drones.

Mick had some good news on the search for aviation footage. Two microlights and a Robinson R22 helicopter had been flying in that area of

Northumberland about the time of the murder. The pilots and passengers of the aircraft were being contacted to see if any recordings were available.

Chapter 24 – Revered former detective

Christine, Robbie and Parrish had enjoyed an evening spent together chatting over their evening meal. Robbie had prepared it and it was another which was gluten-free as he had coeliac disease.

Since the start of his stay, Parrish had mostly eaten with his hosts and had not eaten bread or pasta. He was beginning to feel the benefits and attempted to make a mental note to change his diet when he returned to Helmsley. Remembering the mental note was another matter entirely.

Before he went to bed, he sent a text to DI Morter:

Hi Mick, Apologies for the late text. I need to rest so I'll miss the HM interview. See you after. P

Within a minute he got a reply:

No problem. Get as much rest as you need.

Perhaps Mick was starting to understand ME a little better, hoped Parrish.

It was Tuesday morning and Parrish stayed in bed until after his hosts had left for work. He went through his usual routine and then returned to bed. Occasionally checking the time, he stayed there for as long as possible to get as much rest as he could.

Experience had told him, resting in bed was better for his recovery than lying on a settee or in his recliner and certainly better than sitting up in a chair.

A little before noon, Parrish received another text from DI Morter:

Hi P, HM interview complete. Useful. We can discuss it later. Sturridge due in at 2 pm if you are up to it. Cheers Mick

The thrill of the case caused Parrish to leave the sanctuary of his bed as soon as he had read the text. The decision to shower or not, on the basis of effort expended, went to 'quick shower'. This was followed by another naproxen and a light lunch. He was in police HQ before 1 pm and being debriefed by DI Morter.

Their email request the previous day to Heledd Morgan had been swiftly replied to. They now had a list of possible suspects who had applied for business managers positions and been unsuccessful. This included a dozen members of staff currently working in the HR department.

During the forthcoming interview with Rachel Sturridge, Parrish and DI Morter agreed to encourage her to mention names of HR staff. They would listen intently for names being mentioned and that most definitely included the dozen potential suspects. They fully intended to get information on all twelve names from Rachel by the end of the interview.

Conversation turned to the interview with Heledd Morgan. It had not gone smoothly. She had been reluctant to give information. She had eventually said that it may have been a possibility that some individuals both in HR and the wider university 'may not be on board with current strategy'. This added weight to the theory of a division between colleagues.

DI Morter had cunningly further explored her role in the university. She was happy to explain this and her importance to implementing strategy across the whole university. Similarly, she explained how she had empowered her business managers to manage day-to-day business in HR.

When he suggested that perhaps it was the business managers who really ran HR, she countered him angrily, 'They were implementing her policy'. Her explanation of her role and the angry retort to his suggestion, merely confirmed the likely office power in HR did not lie with her. He continued probing with his questioning and again, although unintentionally, her answers pointed to Charlee Butcher wielding power on day-to-day matters.

The subject of allegations of sexual harassment against Napoleon drew the vehement denial they had expected. Also just as expected, the revelation of names of female employees who may have made allegations brought a change in the demeanour of Morgan. This was especially so when her interview was about to end for their interviews to begin.

Faced with even more potential turmoil at the university and bad press, Heledd Morgan suggested that there had been no formal allegations of such behaviour. She should have recalled from her first meeting with DI Morter that he was familiar with UK employment law. He explained to her, which she knew full well, that a grievance doesn't have to be put in writing on an official form to make it formal. It can simply be spoken to someone recognised by the university's written policy, often any manager, mentor, any HR staff member and numerous other points of contact in an organisation.

Reluctantly, Heledd Morgan had confirmed that this had happened. She had initially let Charlee Butcher deal with the allegations. This meant discreet enquiries and then for her to make the problem go away using thinly veiled threats to the career of the accuser.

However, the number and severity of accusations had resulted in Charlee Butcher raising concerns with her. Heledd had then 'consulted as necessary' with the most senior member of staff at the university, the Vice-Chancellor. This led to a meeting between the Vice-Chancellor, Morgan and Napoleon. He was given little option as to his choices. He was on gardening leave until he found another position elsewhere or he resigned on the spot.

'So, the disgusting little man was on full pay for months until he got another job?'

'Unfortunately, yes. The university hands were tied. If they suspended him on full pay and investigated the allegations, that might have resulted in bad press for them. If they didn't follow written procedure, they couldn't dismiss him for gross misconduct, otherwise they would likely end up with him taking them down the costly employment tribunal route. If that went to conclusion, the hearing conclusions are posted on a Government website for anyone to read, which would be bad press. Gardening leave on full pay was little more costly financially than following procedure. It also minimised revelations in the media and importantly social media. Can you imagine the carnage on social media if they had suspended him, investigated and dismissed him, then handed the cases over to the police?'

'With such a manipulative and morally devoid institution, the likes of Bear and Elfyn had no chance. As a matter of urgency, we need to confirm alibis for the murder of Charlee Butcher or investigate all the women who made allegations and those employees forced out of the university.'

Parrish had unwittingly spoken to the lead investigator as if he was the DCI. DI Morter wasn't going to pull him up on it, he was in full agreement with the revered former detective. Parrish realised immediately what he done, but chose not to apologise.

Chapter 25 – Cake and biscuits

Rachel Sturridge was decidedly nervous when Parrish and DI Morter entered the interview room. DI Morter made the necessary statements for the benefit of the recording. The interview then began, led by Parrish. In a calming reassuring voice, he ostensibly talked about her not needing to worry and to remain calm, although really he was quite happy for her to remain alarmed. From meeting her previously, he felt confident it would lead to her spilling the beans.

It took little effort to get Rachel to admit that disquiet existed amongst most of the university employees. She added substance to the theory of a traditionalist versus modernist split. There were those, like Bear and Elfyn who believed, and had stood up for, the traditional university educational values. Most of these staff members were no longer at the university. Many more employees remained at the university with this view, but had only exchanged it in whispers with the like-minded.

There were many administrative and technical staff, who had been forced to reapply for their jobs. Albeit with an ever so slightly different job title and vastly expanded job description, role and responsibilities. Few had been successful in being employed in the new roles. Fewer still appreciated the burden placed upon them and the new working ethos and environment.

The university upper management had driven this ethos and it was a moot point if this had come from Heledd Morgan and HR, or elsewhere. Crucially, a small hard core of employees had been either moved into new roles or recruited from outside the university and were gleefully enforcing policy on everyone else.

Parrish honed in on HR. In front of him was a hierarchal representation of HR, which he turned so that Rachel could see it too. Heledd Morgan sat at the top of the chart, with the four business managers below. Under three of the business managers were lists of staff appointed to their respective faculty. This information had been provided by Heledd already, as was when they had been appointed at the university, which was written alongside each name.

With various coloured highlighters now placed on the table, he began to quiz Rachel briefly about each staff member. She gave her assumption of whether they were committed to the new cause, or holding older values. With blue, he highlighted those zealously implementing new policy. Those who apparently held strong traditional views were highlighted in green.

Despite looking at this representation and helping him highlight staff members, Rachel Sturridge hadn't noticed very small black marks that Parrish had put against twelve names. These were the failed business manager applicants. There were two of these names now in blue and four in green.

It was the four names highlighted in green that he now asked her about. Unfortunately, other than to confirm that these people held very strong views, Rachel hadn't detected strong animosity towards those awarded the post. Likewise, all did their jobs as instructed.

To emphasise a change in proceedings, Parrish sat back in his chair and puffed out his cheeks as he exhaled. It was all a show. 'Who ran HR on a day-to-day basis Rachel?'

'Heledd. Heledd Morgan the director' and she pointed to the top of the chart.

'No, who ran it on a day-to-day basis?'

Rachel pointed to her business manager, 'I work for Lisa Marshall, HR head of the Art and Humanities faculty.'

With a change of tack, Parrish asked, 'Who made you all wear rainbow-colored lanyards?'

Rachel blushed but answered, 'Charlee Butcher.'

'Would you say she was the de real day-to-day boss of HR?'

'You could probably say that. She was very forceful.'

'Did you know what she did, day-to-day?'

'Not officially, but yes, we all did.'

'And what was that?'

'She worked with Dr Carlang and the Pro V-C on special projects.'

'And what were special projects?'

'I doubt I know the full extent of them. Certainly, they included dealing with difficult students and members of staff.'

'Difficult? Difficult like Dr Elfyn Williams and Dr Bear Lawrence?'

'They weren't in my faculty.'

'But you must have heard about them? Those conversations in the kitchen over a cup of tea maybe?'

Rachel sighed. She had kept little back and was resigned to answering whatever was put to her. 'I did hear about them. Like a number of staff that Charlee dealt with, they seemed to have been treated very unfairly.'

Once again, Parrish acted out a routine to indicate a change of tack. 'The special projects team, Charlee Butcher, Dr Carlang and Professor Vince Cook, did they chat with the other staff? Maybe in the kitchen, in a break, share a coffee with you all?'

'The Pro V-C pretty much spoke only to them and occasionally Heledd. Charlee was private and didn't chat much. Dr Carlang was the opposite. I got the feeling he was a lonely sole.'

'Why do you say that?'

'Well, he was a divorcee and he never talked about any family or friends outside of the university. He supported Embleton United Football Club, I know that. He just chatted over tea or coffee and enjoyed eating cake and scoffing biscuits.'

'Cake and biscuits?'

'Yes, on a Friday, we took turns in the office to bring in biscuits or cake. Everyone was free to eat them. A lot of the new staff just brought in biscuits. Us older ones would either buy a cake or bring in one we had made at home.'

'So, he enjoyed eating cake?'

'Oh yes, very much so. When he was ill in hospital, we talked about maybe taking some in for him.'

'Did you indeed? Did anyone do that?'

'I'm sorry, I don't know. I went off ill for a couple of weeks myself. Mature lady's health issues. You know the sort of thing.'

Parrish wasn't entirely sure that he did know. He had heard of the menopause, but his wife had left him before she experienced it. The full range of debilitating symptoms was unknown to him, plus some of the treatments which could include surgical procedures.

'Could you hazard a guess who might have visited him? Perhaps he chatted to someone more often than the others?'

'Well Barbara and Stacey used to sometimes make tea or coffee for him and each other. He would do likewise for them. I shouldn't say this, but Barbara liked baking cakes and eating them. Stacey was much more health conscious, went to the gym, jogged and the like.'

Turning to his colleague, Parrish asked, 'DI Morter, do you have any more questions for Rachel?'

'No, I don't... Thank you for your time, Rachel.'

With that, DI Morter escorted Rachel out of the building. When he returned to the room, Parrish was surveying the chart used in the interview.

'She gave us a lot of information, but was it useful?' asked DI Morter.

'If you can get the names of everyone who visited Carlang in hospital, it might prove insightful.'

Chapter 26 – Grainy images

DI Morter had worked late with his team into Tuesday night after the interviews. With only a few hours' sleep, he was back in police HQ early the follow morning. His team had made some interesting developments that he was keen to both follow up and share with Parrish when he arrived.

It was late Wednesday morning when Parrish secured the Honda to the bicycle parking outside. The receptionist glared at him as he entered the foyer. Parrish gave her a broad smile then flashed his ID at the electronic door release before entering the bowels of the building.

In the investigation room, Mick and his team were busy working at a number of computers. When Parrish entered, DI Morter introduced him to those present, DS Ash and DC Smith, before briefing him on progress.

The train companies had been surprisingly helpful at providing CCTV recordings from trains that had used the main line during the time window requested. Examining the CCTV train footage had brought challenges to the investigative team. Unsurprisingly, none of them had driven a train and spent hours looking along a train line.

Identifying stations, quickly reduced the length of footage they needed to consider. Identifying the line crossings helped again. They were looking at five crossings initially, which were called; Brunton North, Brunton South, Fallodon, Christon Bank and Cock Law.

Blurry images from a high-speed train led them to identify a suspect dressed in dark clothing. The person was approximately one hundred metres south of the Fallodon crossing. This recording had been passed on to specialist officers trained in digital image enhancement techniques. Meanwhile, the team poured over the footage, time and time again, to see what additional information may come to light.

There was about two hours of footage to go through from one of the microlights and the R22 helicopter. None of the investigative team were pilots and as with the train CCTV, they soon realised that they were unfamiliar with the aerial view of Northumberland they were looking at. The microlight had generally flown higher and the helicopter lower, as was normal for these aircraft. This had led the team to concentrate on the helicopter imagery first. It took time to understand what they were looking at using the satellite view from Google maps. Eventually, they were able to break the footage into sections, which contained images of the area they were interested in.

They had a description and pictures of Charlee Butcher. With blond hair and a purple outfit, she was the first person of interest spotted on the aerial footage. This new information gave them a more detailed and accurate knowledge of the route she had followed from Embleton.

She had run south towards Cock Law, before heading north towards Christon Bank and Fallodon Hall. There were very few other people spotted along the route. Previously, the investigation had identified some other people in the area. These had given witness statements and the police had recorded what they too were wearing. So far, no further possible suspect could be seen.

The team now re-examined the footage, widening their search. They had been instructed to consider what had been in the north east area of the original investigation search area, suggested by Parrish. It had been made clear to them to search the railway line crossings too.

Grainy, pixelated images of a figure in dark clothes revealed a possible suspect. The figure came into view from woodland and had stopped parallel to the railway line as a train passed. The figure was about one hundred metres south of the Fallodon crossing. Again, the recording was passed on to be the appropriate specialist officers, whilst the team continued to scour the footage. They had a match with the train CCTV and also with DCI Parrish's theory.

Overhead drone searches of the railway line had already started north of the previously searched area near Christon Bank. The drone search team had been slowly working north along the course of the tracks.

It was slow going for a number of reasons, not least to be thorough. They had over a kilometre and a half, nearly one mile of tracks, to cover. When the team at HQ identified the possible suspect using the train footage, they quickly contacted the drone team to relocate the search. The drone team moved location to one hundred metres south of the Fallodon crossing on the west side of the tracks.

Soon, the long-range lens of the drone was zooming in on a small, black, rectangular object on the tracks. They were fairly certain that they had identified a phone. The phone appeared whole, although the screen was face down and could be broken. Even if it wasn't, would they be able to retrieve data from the phone after it had been exposed to Northumberland weather for months? The bigger question was, had it belonged to Charlee Butcher? Arrangements were started with Network Rail to retrieve the phone from the tracks, as soon as possible. It would involve a lot of co-ordination and a mountain of paperwork.

After Parrish had been briefed by DI Morter on the latest developments in the investigation, he decided to stay in the investigation room. He had often done this when he worked for the Met. It had been a morale booster for the staff working on the case to see the boss on the shop floor. Since he had joined this case as a guest, he had usually retired to bed at his hosts after a meeting or interview. Guest he maybe, but he understood the faith that had been placed in him. He could not ignore that resources were being put into the investigation as a result of his efforts.

Only yesterday, Parrish had spoken to DI Morter as if he was the DCI on this patch. DCI Alexanderson was in charge, but from day-to-day it had almost become Parrish who was in charge. It was an uncomfortable parallel to draw with Charlee Butcher. But still he stayed to support those working on the case in the investigation room.

His thoughts turned back to the interview with Rachel Sturridge. He fetched the highlighted chart from the interview showing the HR hierarchy. Beside it he lay the sketch of the HR office layout with the staff names. Despite the belief that the killer was a man, Parrish couldn't ignore his gut feeling that the killer came from within HR.

In the interview, Parrish had used two different coloured highlighters. Blue marked those staff supportive of the new regime in HR. Green marked those who weren't. He wasn't interested in those marked in blue, they would have little reason to hate Charlee Butcher. Those in green just might.

Using the green marker again, he used it to highlight on the layout sketch those in green on the hierarchy chart. *What did that mean?* He asked himself. Using his imagination and the layout of the investigation room, he began to sit in different seats in his mind. *What did each person see from their desk?*

One of Parrish's favourite films was Hannibal, with Anthony Hopkins. There was a line from the film that had struck a chord with the young Parrish in his early days as a detective. He couldn't remember the exact words from the movie, but it didn't matter, he understood the meaning of the phrase and it was true.

'We covet what we see.'

It means that we begin to desire what we see regularly. Advertisers know this all too well. People buy what they repeatedly see advertised. Killers, murder those they see regularly too, just as Hannibal Lecter had told Clarice. *Who was looking at Charlee Butcher?*

Four people had been highlighted in green on the hierarchy chart. Two of these were highlighted in green on the layout chart and faced Charlee Butcher's office. His memory was failing him. *Had he heard their names before and if so, where and when?*

'Mick, sorry to bother you, do you have a minute?' asked Parrish.

'Sure.' DI Morter got up from his chair and walked over to Parrish.

'Take a look at these two names, please. Do you recognise them?'

'Can't be one hundred percent, but didn't Rachel Sturridge mention a Barbara and Stacey in the interview?'

'That's it! You beauty! Where can I watch and listen to the interview again?'

'On your laptop, it's been uploaded to the database. I'll fetch you some headphones so you don't disturb the team whilst you listen to it.'

'Would you like a coffee and where do I get some?'

'Down the hallway, turn left, there is a machine. I'm good, thanks.'

There was a water dispenser next to the coffee machine. Parrish took the opportunity to swallow a naproxen and cancel the upcoming alarm on his phone so as not to disturb the others when he returned to the office. It was a fancy-looking coffee machine, with claims of 'fresh coffee' on it in big letters. He had high hopes for his brew. He took a sip and thought to himself, *granulated coffee rehydrated in water.*

Back in the office, the disappointing coffee at least had the effect that the wanted, he was sated and energised. With the interview located in the database and the earphones on his head, he got himself comfortable in the chair and began to watch the recording.

Some of the interview he couldn't remember. In the early years of having ME, Parrish was often worried, even terrified, that his memory repeatedly failed him. The worry gradually turned to grief over the months and years as he realized he had lost his old self. More time passed and he began to accept his new self with its limitations. Unable to do much of the physical activities he once did, he tried to find joy in even the smallest things in life. Now, the poor memory didn't concern him, *it is what it is,* he thought briefly as he followed the recording.

It was towards the end of the interview when he found what he was looking for. Rachel had indeed mentioned a Barbara and Stacey. He paused the recording and looked at the HR layout sketch. There they were, Barbara Dowson and Stacey Richards.

Initially, Parrish was pleased at this discovery as it meant both women had desks, which positioned them with a good view of Charlee Butcher's office. However, he was slightly disappointed that they weren't directly looking at her office. They were positioned closer to Dr Carlang's office.

He re-played that part of the interview with Rachel answering his questions.

'Well Barbara and Stacey used to sometimes make tea or coffee for him and each other. He would do likewise for them.'

Could one of these women have killed both Butcher and Carlang? He wondered. The recording continued,

'I shouldn't say this, but Barbara liked baking cakes and eating them. Stacey was much more health conscious, went to the gym, jogged and the like.'

If one of these women did kill Butcher, it had to be Stacey Richards, thought Parrish. *She went to the gym, jogged and was health conscious. The investigation has assumed a man had killed Butcher. But could a strong, athletic woman have killed her?* wondered Parrish, *probably with adrenaline pumping through her veins.*

Chapter 27 – Gnawing feeling

Although Parrish had potentially identified the killer, he decided against telling Mick just yet. The investigation to date was insistent that the killer was male and Parrish considered it a possibility that it was a woman.

Another thorny issue for Parrish was, *how was Carlang murdered, if indeed he was?* He had died in hospital under circumstances not considered suspicious. Access to the data held on Carlang might help him solve this, but he was currently denied it.

The deal Parrish had struck with DI Morter was access to the information on both Carlang and Natasha Horseman, if he could find Charlee Butcher's phone. The search had found a phone, but they didn't know yet if it was hers. He didn't have the bargaining power that he needed.

After bidding the team in police HQ goodbye and arranging to catch up with Mick the next day, Parrish headed back to his temporary home. When he got back, Christine was home in the kitchen.

'Hi P, I'm just fixing myself a milkshake. Would you like one, a coffee or something stronger perhaps?'

'It's a bit early really, but I think I've earned the right to a glass of vino.'

'Well, you know what they say, if the sun's gone past the yardarm it's time for a drink. What would you like?'

'White please?'

'Pinot, chardonnay or sauvignon?'

'As long as it's white and chilled, I'm happy.'

Christine took a bottle of pinot grigio from the fridge and poured him a large glass of wine. She passed it to him and he thanked her as he took it. Parrish took a sip and savoured the cool, refreshing tang of the Italian wine.

He sat and chatted as she prepared the milkshake. She scooped ice-cream into a blender then drenched milk in too. Then she carefully added a shot of vanilla syrup before blitzing the mixture in the blender. He liked the look and the idea of milk-shakes, but he had never enjoyed drinking one.

When they had both finished their drinks, Christine went upstairs to get ready for later that evening. After Robbie got home, the three of them were going to a local restaurant for a meal.

Parrish decided he would relax for a few minutes before he freshened up to go out. For the second time that day, something was gnawing away at him, but he couldn't grasp what it was. He resolved to try and relax, stop thinking about the case and enjoy a pleasant evening with his friends.

The next morning, despite sleeping relatively well for a change, Parrish still felt unrested, aching and fatigued. He lay in bed and that gnawing feeling was back in his mind. What was it that he wasn't seeing? He decided to get up and join his hosts for breakfast for a change.

'Coffee, black, no sugar?' asked Robbie.

'Yes please, Sir,' replied Parrish.

Parrish took a seat at the dining table and watched Robbie fill a mug with coffee from a drip machine. Robbie passed this to Parrish unselfishly and began to make one for himself. Sat in a half-sleepy daydream, Parrish watched Robbie fill another mug with coffee. From the fridge, Robbie fetched milk, which he poured into the mug. Next, he added a spoonful of sugar.

Parrish felt like he had been hit with an electric cattle prod and jerked upright in his chair. The gnawing feeling had gone, where was the laptop? It was still in the living room on charge where he picked it up and fired it into life. 'Come on, come on,' he muttered at the recalcitrant machine.

'Everything OK?' shouted Robbie from the kitchen diner.

'Oh, yes, sorry, just had an idea and need to check something out on the laptop.'

When the laptop finally began co-operating, Parrish opened the interview again that he had been watching yesterday. He scrolled through until he found what he wanted to review.

'He supported Embleton United Football Club…' Rachel had said in the interview.

Because he had an Embleton United mug and coaster, it was in the box SOCO took from his office, recalled Parrish.

'…he just chatted over tea or coffee and enjoyed eating cake and scoffing biscuits … we took turns in the office to bring in biscuits or cake … us older ones would either buy a cake or bring in one we had made at home … when he was ill in hospital, we talked about maybe taking some in for him… Barbara and Stacey used to sometimes make tea or coffee for him and each other. He would do likewise for them.'

The night before, Parrish had watched Christine add a shot of syrup to flavour a milkshake. This morning, he had watched Robbie add sugar to a cup of coffee. The sight of the sugar being added to the coffee had unlocked the gnawing in his head. *Had Carlang been poisoned over time in the office, through drinking tea or coffee? Had it been from eating poisoned cake? Had anyone visited him in hospital and poisoned him?*

Chapter 28 – Would I do that?

Hi Mick, are you in HQ and free if I pop over this morning? P

The reply to Parrish's text was swift

Yes, and I always have time to listen to you Mr P.

Parrish was used to waking up feeling like it was Groundhog Day. The pain, fatigue and numerous other symptoms such as his tinnitus, which he really, really didn't enjoy. Not good, not good at all.

But he had a new part to his current Groundhog Day, which he rather enjoyed. After securing the scooter to a bicycle bay again, he entered the foyer of the police HQ. The same receptionist glared the same glare she gave Parrish every time he parked his scooter there.

'Good morning! You're looking radiant today! Have a nice day!' he chirped as he entered the secured part of the building. The receptionist did not reply. The glare turned into a scowl. *Yes!* Thought Parrish, *an enjoyable element added to my Groundhog Day!*

DI Morter was working at a computer in the interview room when Parrish walked through the doorway. After saying hello to each other, Parrish suggested they move to Mick's office to have a chat.

'What's up?' asked DI Morter curiously.

'Just hoping you could bring me up to speed on the investigation,' replied Parrish innocuously.

As Parrish had never previously suggested that they talk in private in his office, DI Morter was suspicious that Parrish may have an ulterior motive for doing so. He decided to update Parrish and wait to hear what was really afoot.

The investigation team were still waiting on the enhanced images of the suspect from both the train and helicopter recordings. The overhead footage had provided a glimpse of what they believed to be the same suspect, further along the footpath. Now attention turned to the mammoth amount of CCTV they had from Embleton, to see if they could pick up the suspect there. Mick didn't need to tell Parrish the size of this task.

The phone had been retrieved and both the IMEI and serial numbers on it confirmed that it was Charlee Butcher's phone. As it had been a recent model, it was IP68 rated and effectively waterproof when left outside. Butcher had used a lock on her phone, which would have likely prevented the killer from accessing it. The investigation was tentatively accepting this scenario as a possible explanation for the killer throwing the phone onto the railway tracks. The reason for doing so, may also have been to prevent the phone being found and, or, to damage or destroy it. Nevertheless, the forensic specialists had easily gained access to the contents once they received it.

'Very little of interest has come to light, so far, but it takes time. Looks like she regularly deleted messages, texts, emails and the like. We'll probably be able to retrieve those too unless she had specialist knowledge on how to erase them completely.'

'That's good progress. Would you pass on my gratitude to the team?'

'Of course.'

'There were a few lines of enquiry that we have also discussed previously; the women who had made allegations of sexual harassment, other potential suspects forced out of the university, etc. Can I ask though, have we had any success regarding visitors to see Carlang in hospital?'

'You know that we are accepting the medical opinion that it wasn't a suspicious death.'

'I do. Doesn't stop me having a look through those and any other information held on the database, does it?'

'OK, OK. We had a deal, right. We've found the phone with your help, thank you. I'll arrange for you to have access to those parts of the database. But please Mr P, don't go making big noises on these. I'll get a hell of a lot of grief from my DCI if you do.'

'Would I do that?'

Mick grimaced, shook his head and the meeting was over.

Back at his temporary home and with the scooter locked securely in the garage, Parrish sat in an armchair in the living room and powered up the laptop. When he eventually logged on, the IT admin team back at police HQ had already activated his access to Carlang and Horseman on the database.

His primary interest was to investigate the death of Dr Carlang. Many murders are committed by the spouse or partner of the deceased and Parrish already knew that Carlang was a single divorcee. Another commonly observed murder trait is that the killer often 'finds' the body or leads the police to it. Likewise, they are frequently in the vicinity of the body when SOCO and other police are present. A seemingly large number of killers also attend the funerals of their victims. *Carlang died in hospital, surrounded by medical staff. Although possible, it was unlikely one was his killer*, thought Parrish. There was no police investigation as a consequence.

Knowing all of these, Parrish couldn't help himself but take a quick peek at the Horseman case first, which had been investigated. He started with the summary of the investigation. Natasha Horseman had died from blunt trauma as a result of the fall from the cliffs. If she had been bludgeoned but not killed before her fall, the pathologist was unable to say. If this had happened, it was now unidentifiable from the considerable trauma as a result of the fall.

There had been some bruising to her arms and back, which could have been from someone pushing her off the cliff. The problem with this theory was that when her partner, Gary, was interviewed, he admitted to a volatile and physical relationship. This was true both sexually and in disagreements. Gary claimed that he and Natasha had fought and had rough sex to make up, earlier that week, which could have resulted in the bruising.

What was even more unfortunate was that Gary had a water-tight alibi for the time when Natasha died. Her body had been found on the Saturday morning by the manager of Dunstanburgh Castle and she had died the previous day. The pathologist had estimated the death to be approximately between 4 pm and 6 pm, on the Friday.

At the start of this timeframe, Gary had been working, doing deliveries. Then he had driven home and gone to the pub with his mates. He had lots of witnesses to his movements, some data-logs for deliveries and his work. The investigation had pulled up ANPR for his work vehicle and his own car, which matched his witness statement. CCTV had also captured him in the pub.

The police investigation had considered who had motive and opportunity. Gary had been the initial suspect but was quickly ruled out. Devon Clarke, who found the body, had also been considered but the investigation, such that it was, had not found any connection to Horseman.

The body of Natasha Horseman was still clothed when it was found. Both her phone and her purse were still in her coat so theft was ruled out. All other lines of enquiry had also come to nought. This niggled Parrish, given what had come to light since his time working on the Charlee Butcher case. *Too few resources to do a proper job*, he thought.

Armed with the knowledge of his own research into the death of Natasha Horseman, Parrish examined the file for financial details of her life. Nothing untoward had come up. With Gary having been swiftly eliminated, his finances had been given only a cursory examination, but they seemed in order too.

Parrish was about to stop wasting his time with this death and move on to Carlang. Before he did, he decided to read the witness statement of Devon Clarke. What he read piqued his interest, so he dug a little deeper.

Chapter 29 – A mugs game

The arrival of Robbie back home from work had caused Parrish to stop researching into the death of Natasha Horseman. It was a blessing in disguise as he realised that a number of symptoms such as IBS, tinnitus, joint pain, brain fog and fatigue were getting worse. So, after dinner, Parrish bid his hosts good night and took an early night.

On Friday morning, Parrish once again stayed in bed until Robbie and Christine had both left for work. He decided against a shower after his morning routine of breakfast and meds, and resumed his research.

Yesterday had been interesting looking into the death of Horseman and he definitely felt that he had good cause to investigate further. However, the case in hand was the murder of Charlee Butcher and Parrish had a strong feeling that the demise of Dr Carlang was linked to her murder. If he could uncover what had really happened to Dr Carlang, then he might find the killer of both of them.

After the laptop finally agreed to play ball, Parrish discovered that there was very little information in the database on the death of Carlang, as he had suspected. Carlang was 46 years old, obese and had been admitted to hospital with chest pains. He had died several days later, still in hospital, of a heart attack. A doctor had pronounced him dead and it was not considered a suspicious death. Consequently, the coroner had not been involved. There had been no post-mortem, neither invasive nor non-invasive and no blood tests. Worse still for Parrish, who held suspicions that Carlang may have been poisoned, was that Carlang had been cremated. There was no body left to examine.

The staff in HR had made statements in relation to Charlee Butcher's murder. Parrish now searched these using 'Carlang' as the search term.

No search results.

All he had on Carlang was from the interview with Rachel Sturridge. She had mentioned that Barbara and Stacey from HR had sometimes made coffee for Carlang, plus they brought in cakes, for the office staff. Carlang had apparently been quite fond of a piece of cake.

If Carlang was poisoned, how was it done? wondered Parrish. *It couldn't have been through a large cake, sliced up for all to eat, unless the poisoner wanted all the staff dead and had abstained from eating their own cake.*

Perhaps the poisoner had brought in many small individual cakes. This allowed the possibility of administering poison to one cake. But that would have been difficult to ensure that Carlang ate it and nobody else.

So, was the poison in the coffee? The staff kitchen would provide enough privacy to add poison to a cup of coffee and target Carlang. But presumably the killer then had to be careful who drank, which cup. Not that hard though, especially if they had their own cup or mug.

And Carlang did have his own mug, realised Parrish suddenly. *Rachel had mentioned that Carlang supported Embleton United and Carlang had an Embleton United mug and coaster. It was in the box of his personal effects that SOCO had examined.*

SOCO had examined the mug and coaster for fingerprints and DNA. But had they run any toxicology tests? Parrish searched the database and could find nothing. *Definitely worth running the tests*, thought Parrish.

What am I thinking about? Thought Parrish to himself. *Carlang died in hospital several days later. Could a poisoned coffee have killed him several days later?* He couldn't answer that.

But where was Carlang when he had the chest pains? Parrish suddenly thought. He searched through the information to find the ambulance report. *Carlang had been in HR in the University!*

Is this the break-through I'm looking for? he asked himself. *Possibly, but if I can find out who had visited*

Carlang in hospital, that might add weight to his theory. It would if it were Barbara or Stacey and especially if it was the athletic Stacey.

The information on Dr Carlang in the police database was sparse and there were no logs or lists of hospital visitors. Still using the laptop, Parrish brought up the website for Embleton Hospital and then the Cardiology Department. There was lots of information about the department, but nothing about visitor logs. Phone numbers were provided for various services and Parrish decided to ring the critical care number.

'Critical care.'

'Hi, this is DCI Parrish from Northumberland and Cheviots Police Force murder team. Would you please tell me if you keep visitor logs to your department?'

'We keep logs of staff and patients, but not for visitors.'

'How might I know if someone had visited a patient?'

'Have you asked the patient?'

'They're dead.'

'Friends or family?'

'Would staff know?'

'I doubt it, we're very busy. Have you asked security if they can help?'

'That's next on my list.'

Parrish rang the main switchboard and after waiting the best part of twenty minutes, finally got through. His call was quickly put through to the main security office. The security officer who answered the call was only too eager to help what he thought was a murder investigation rather than deal with parking fine complaints. He explained that they had CCTV in a number of public areas.

After talking it through, the security officer agreed to forward recordings through to Parrish. Initially, he wanted to send as much as he had, but Parrish said that would only be necessary in the fullness of time. For now, the security officer would forward that for the public area outside the entrance that led to the Acute Cardiology Unit for the visitor times on the dates Dr Carlang was in hospital, which Parrish provided.

When the security officer asked for Parrish for his email address, Parrish gave him the temporary email address he had been given by the police IT department. Within an hour, several emails arrived, each containing a compressed file containing the recordings.

With so much video to potentially view, Parrish decided to start on the last visiting time before the death of Carlang. His plan was to work backwards from there until, hopefully, he found the killer. Before he started, he refreshed his memory with the images of Barbara and Stacey that were stored in the police database.

The final visiting time before the demise of Carlang was from 3:30 pm until 6:30 pm. Parrish quickly got the hang of watching speeded up footage, then stopping and rewinding when he saw something interesting. He got to the end of this visiting time and had found nothing of interest. Noticing the time, Parrish got up and went through to the kitchen to help himself to a coffee and to swallow another naproxen with some cold water.

Back in the living room with his coffee, Parrish started watching the video from earlier that same day, 12:30 pm until 3:30 pm. *The lunchtime visiting times were much less busy. Most people were at work*, thought Parrish to himself.

It didn't take him long before he stopped and rewound an interesting piece of footage. The figure mostly had their back to the camera as they approached the door. Not that familiar with Stacey, having only one picture to go on, Parrish thought that it might possibly be her as she turned to enter the doorway. She was also carrying a plastic bag. *What's in there, cake?* wondered Parrish.

Now, he fast-forwarded the recording, hoping she had been captured on film again. It didn't take him long to see her again. This time she was facing the camera as she left the unit. He was sure it was her and she wasn't carrying a bag.

With the laptop safely secured in the under-seat compartment of the Forza, Parrish headed to Police HQ. He found DI Morter in the investigation room and nodded towards the lead investigators office when their eyes met.

'What have you got for me?' asked Mick.

'I know you didn't want me to look into the Carlang and Horseman deaths, but I have. You are going to have to hear me out on these. I think Carlang was poisoned by Stacey Richards who works in HR.'

'Well, I never saw that coming. How would we ever prove such a theory? We have no evidence and Carlang has been cremated.'

'Remember the interview with Rachel from HR? She said that Barbara and Stacey used to make coffee for Carlang occasionally and vice versa. Also, they used to bring in homemade cake to share.'

Mick nodded.

'We can't prove that he was poisoned by eating cake, but we may be able to prove that he had drunk poisoned coffee.'

'How?'

'We run toxicology tests on Carlang's mug and coaster that SOCO retrieved from his HR office.'

'I will arrange for that to be done, but he died in hospital several days after being admitted to hospital.'

'I know. Take a look at this.'

Parrish had opened his laptop as soon as they had sat down in DI Morter's office. It had finally come to life and Parrish was bringing up the files from hospital security. 'This is CCTV footage of the doorway that leads to the Acute Cardiology Unit where Carlang was on the day he died. I believe this is Stacey Richards entering the area and carrying a bag.'

DI Morter frowned with interest at the screen. He was unfamiliar with the picture of Stacey Richards. But the brief glance at the woman on the screen as she turned to enter the doorway brought a feeling of familiarity to him. 'Do you have any better footage?' he asked eagerly.

'Yes, give me a second.'

Parrish angled the laptop towards himself again and forwarded to the next clip he wanted to show his colleague. 'Here it is. Half an hour later, she's leaving without the bag.'

'You need to look at this,' said Mick to Parrish.

Mick clicked at his mouse as he worked his desktop PC. When he found what he wanted, he swung the screen around towards Parrish. It was the enhanced image taken from the train CCTV. Although it was a grainy image, it was the same woman in the hospital. It was Stacey Richards.

DI Morter jumped out of his chair and strode into the open plan investigation room, with Parrish following on behind rather more sedately. 'Please listen in everyone' he said loudly to all the detectives beavering away on the investigation. 'I know it's POETS day, but we have a new prime suspect. Stacey Richards from Embleton HR.'

'I thought we were looking for a male suspect?' asked DS Ash.

'We were. DCI Parrish has been looking into the death of Dr Carlang, as he has always suspected foul play. Our colleague here has a theory that Richards may have been poisoning Carlang's coffee or cake in HR and she may have also poisoned him when he was in hospital. DCI Parrish has uncovered CCTV footage of who we believe to be Stacey Richards in Embleton Hospital near the Acute Cardiology Unit on the day Carlang died. The images of that woman look like the enhanced imagery from the train CCTV of the suspect in dark grey near the Fallodon train crossing.'

DI Morter paused deliberately and a collective murmur could be heard from the assembled troops.

'DC Smith, arrange toxicology examinations of Carlang's mug and coaster taken by SOCO from his HR office. Tell the lab boys it's urgent and prepare warrants to search her home, car, office, beach hut, caravan, wherever she may have hidden evidence.'

The detective constable nodded and scribbled a note on his pad.

'DC Walker, pull the usual on her, phone, bank, the lot. As a priority, I want us to look at where her phone has been. Liaise with DS Ash. She already has Charlee Butcher's routes when she went running in the weeks prior to the murder. We know this was a premeditated murder. Is there any correlation with Stacey Richards movements? The killer knew Butcher and knew she would be running at that time, at that location.'

DC Walker and DS Ash glanced in acknowledgement at each other.

'DS Ash, how are we getting on with the CCTV tracking of the suspect in dark grey clothing returning from the railway crossing to Embleton?'

'It's been slow going, but I'll use the address of Stacey Richards to hopefully let us home in much more quickly on the route she likely took.'

'OK team. This is the best line of enquiry we've had so far. Please cancel your plans for the weekend. I want evidence as soon as possible that supports arresting her and searching her property. If she has killed twice, then Professor Vince Cook can be considered to be in imminent danger so I'll arrange for uniform to watch his home. Thank you everyone. Let's catch this killer.'

Chapter 30 – Almost unique

The two weeks were up. Parrish should have finished offering his insight into the case and returned to Helmsley. By rights he should be laid in bed at home recuperating for days or even weeks after his exertions over the last fortnight. But he was running on adrenaline, they were closing in on the killer. When he eventually hit the wall, he knew he was in for a big crash.

Christine and Robbie were surprised to see him still at their home, although he was always welcome. The fact he was still there spoke volumes that he must have done some first-rate sleuthing. They also knew that he wasn't allowed to tell them what was going on. But they were itching to know.

'OK, I'll offer you a snippet because it was Robbie here who first suspected that foul play was at hand in the deaths of Natasha Horseman and Dr Carlang. I'm convinced the death of Natasha needs looking into further, but quite how it links to Charlee Butcher's murder I'm yet to uncover, if indeed it does.

'The death of Carlang is another matter altogether. I've uncovered grounds to suggest that his death is both suspicious and linked to the murder of Charlee

Butcher. There is a lot of investigative work to do but the team at police HQ are working on it as we speak.'

'How very exciting!' exclaimed Christine.

'What's your next move, Scratcher?' asked Robbie.

'I am off to bed...Good night!'

* * *

Not only was Parrish fatigued, as was normal for him, he was also tired from his work on the investigation. It was almost lunchtime on Saturday when he finally awoke after nearly twelve hours of disturbed sleep. His hosts were home and had been reading quietly in the living room that morning so as not to disturb their sleeping guest.

The three of them chatted whilst Parrish ate a late breakfast. They made plans for the evening, the three of them were heading to a cocktail bar and then on to an Italian restaurant, both in Embleton town centre. After finishing his breakfast and meds, Parrish returned to bed, but not before assuring them that he was recuperating and not sleeping, so that they might enjoy a more usual Saturday. As Parrish lay down in the guest room, he heard 'My Favourite Game' by The Cardigans begin to play.

The music couldn't stop tired Parrish dozing on and off for another six hours before he dragged himself out of bed and into the shower. Before becoming ill,

Parrish had showered at least once a day, sometimes more. Once chronically ill, he had battled for a couple of years attempting to maintain the same routine. Now, he was happy to shower every other day, sometimes less frequently if necessary to save the energy showering demanded. With a good wash and a spray of deodorant, he didn't feel any less clean than if he'd showered.

Sat on the edge of the bed in the guest bedroom, Parrish was busy dressing. Pain in his lower joints demanded he sat to put on his lower garments. As he grimaced putting a foot into his best jeans, his phone pinged. It was a text from DI Morter.

Major developments. Ring whenever it is convenient.

Parrish wasted no time in calling.

'Hi Mr P, we've got the toxicology report back. The mug was clean, but the coaster wasn't. The lab found a cocktail of prescription drugs. We've also got phone traces linking Richards movements to Butcher's routes running near Fallodon prior to the murder.'

'That's fabulous. What's the plan from here?'

'We're going to arrest Stacey Richards, her husband and son at dawn tomorrow. Stacey Richards hasn't been prescribed anything other than anti-biotics in years. But the husband is on a lot of medication and the son is on medication for asthma, anxiety and depression.'

'Potentially, they could all be involved, but I doubt it.'

'So do I. We'll interview the husband and son before we interview Stacey. It also gives us time to shake the house and cars down, plus examine phones and laptops, you know the routine.'

'I do indeed. On that basis, I'll come to HQ mid-morning unless you ring me to do otherwise.'

'Enjoy whatever it is you plan to do in the meantime.'

'Certainly will, cocktails and then a meal with Robbie and Christine.'

'Sounds good. Another couple of hours here then I'll get my head down to be ready for the raid.'

'See you tomorrow. Good luck!'

Chapter 31 – Interview room one

It was mid-morning when Parrish walked into the investigation room. Most of the team were beavering away at computers as usual, examining digital forensics such as bank and bank accounts, or looking through CCTV footage. DS Ash was with DI Morter in his office. Parrish knocked on the door and Mick waved him to come in.

'Good morning to you both,' smiled Parrish.

'Morning, Sir,' replied DS Heather Ash.

'Good morning,' said Mick. 'DS Ash has not long finished interviewing the husband, Andy Richards.'

Parrish turned to look at DS Ash and asked, 'and how did that go?'

'I very much doubt he knew anything about the murders, let alone contributed in anyway. He obviously didn't have access to the HR department to poison Carlang and he's not on the hospital CCTV. We're checking his alibi and movements relating to the Charlee Butcher murder. So far, nothing to link him on that either.'

DI Morter continued, 'DC Smith led the interview of the son, Matthew. Looks like he's not been involved either. Stacey usually ordered the repeat prescriptions for both her husband and son. She had access to all of the various medications found on the coaster. I discussed the medications with the pathologist to more fully understand what may have happened. Andy was on lisinopril to reduce his blood pressure. Matthew was on propranolol for his anxiety, but it's also used to treat high blood pressure. The combination of lisinopril and propranolol together would have been very powerful.

'Large fluctuations in blood pressure are very dangerous and can lead to strokes and heart attacks. After drinking the doctored coffee, he would have experienced a large reduction in blood pressure. After the effects wore off, his blood pressure would rise again. Carlang worked part-time in HR so any poisoning through his coffee would be irregular, which increases the danger compared to taking these medicines regularly.

'She may have dosed him for months, which eventually caused the chest pains and his admittance to hospital. We'll never know, unless she admits it, but whatever she took into the hospital was enough to kill him.'

'That's a good theory, but those are two commonly described medications. Unless she admits to it, the CPS wouldn't find that sufficient evidence to go to court. If we checked, we'd find other staff in HR with access to those medications.'

'You're right to say that. However, the pathologist said that the toxicology report matches the medication that both the husband and son are on. If we look into that particular combination of medication further, the probability of the same being prescribed to another family of someone in HR would be very low.'

'Almost like having unique fingerprints or DNA?'

'Exactly.'

'What's next?' asked Parrish.

'I suggest that we take an early lunch so that we can build our energy for interviewing Stacey Richards. I'll tell you what we have found at the house and on her phone so far. It will also give the team more time to work through the forensics too. And if you will forgive me the pun, whilst we dine, Stacey Richards can stew.'

Stacey Richards had been marched from the cell to interview room one by the two largest policemen that had been available in police HQ. The hours waiting in the cell and the tall policemen had been deliberate. Whilst she was suspected to be a double-murderer, she had no criminal record. The hope was the intimidation and unfamiliarity with the process and her surroundings would make her slip up at interview, or even cave in and admit her wrong-doing.

She had declined the offer of a solicitor and was sat on a chair opposite DI Morter. Between them was a desk where a laptop sat open in front of DI Morter. DS Ash sat to one side so that the desk was not between her and Stacey Richards. It was a deliberate ploy so that the two females might bond during the interview. Stacey might then be more inclined to trust in 'good cop' DS Ash and reveal important information.

DCI Parrish watched a live feed of the interview on his loaned laptop whilst sat in the investigation room. He knew that Stacey Richards had been arrested for the murder of Charlee Butcher, without any mention of the death of Dr Carlang. The interview team were keeping that up their sleeves to apply pressure later during the interview.

The interview began after DI Morter made formal introductions and made the necessary statements for the recording. It was DS Ash who began the interview. 'Where were you between 4 pm and 6 pm on Monday April 17th?'

'That's a long time ago now, it's difficult to remember.'

DI Morter interjected, it was sooner than he and DS Ash had hoped, but he had his role to play as 'bad cop' in the interview, 'Let me focus your attention. That was when Charlee Butcher, your former colleague, was brutally murdered in woods near Fallodon Hall.'

'I'll have been to work and then gone home or to the gym.'

DS Ash stated, 'you said in your witness statement taken a few days after the body was found, that you went home, where you stayed until leaving for work the next morning.'

'Yes, that's what I did. I went home and cooked a meal for Andy and Matthew.'

'Earlier today, I interviewed your husband and he said that when he got home that evening, you weren't there. He said you came home later after being out running.'

'He wouldn't have said that because it's not true. Just ask Matthew, he'll back me up.'

'They've both been interviewed separately and both of them have confirmed you had been out running.'

'You're lying! They wouldn't say that, it's not true.'

'I'm afraid it is true,' said DI Morter, 'when they were made aware of certain facts known to us and that perverting the course of justice is a criminal offence, they both confirmed that you were not home at the time Charlee Butcher was murdered.'

The interview was choreographed. Stacey Richards had no alibi now. The two detectives would now walk her through preparations for the murder. DS Ash resumed the interrogation calmly. 'When the clocks went forward an hour in late March, it was light enough to go for a run on an evening. Charlee Butcher started running into rural Northumberland every Monday after work when the clocks changed. We know this from tracking the course of her phone as it pinged off various telecommunication masts. But you know that don't you?'

'I don't know that.'

'We have tracked the movements of your phone the weeks after the clocks went forward. You're a good runner, aren't you? You followed Charlee Butcher on her runs on the first two Monday evenings after the clocks changed. On the third week, you took a different route and waited whilst she ran by you, hidden in woodland. The next week, you did the same, except you didn't have your phone with you and you murdered her.'

'I didn't!'

'Didn't what? Follow her? Wait for her? Murder her?' asked DI Morter sternly.

'None of it!'

Stacey was rattled. The interview was going well. The 'bad cop' DI Morter would stay quiet now, whilst 'good cop', DS Ash resumed the interview. 'You and Charlee both went to a gym and both were runners. You were both athletic. You will have chatted about where you went to the gym. You will have talked about where you went running. She told you that she would be running cross-country on a Monday night. You left work before her and waited for her near her home. When she left her home to go on her run, you followed her.'

The two detectives had been highly trained in interview techniques. They saw the ticks that revealed to them that Stacey Richards was decidedly uncomfortable with the interview.

'How would I possibly know that? I worked in the same department as her, but we didn't work together. She didn't chat to any of us.'

Stacey Richards was giving more than visual clues to her guilt. She had asked a question, desperate for information. The rule for interrogators is that they ask the questions, not the suspect. Ignoring the question, DS Ash probed a little deeper. 'Who do you mean by 'us'?'

'The office staff, those of us who sit in the main office. Not the managers in their glass-fronted offices,' spat Stacey.

'You weren't a fan of Charlee Butcher then?'

'Not really, if I'm honest. She thought she was the boss.'

'Why do you say that, what sort of things did she do?'

'She made us all wear rainbow lanyards for a start.'

'The same rainbow lanyard that was used to choke her to death?' asked DI Morter firmly.

'They said on the news that the ligature hadn't been found.'

'How did it feel strangling her to death? Did you enjoy it? Did she deserve it?'

'No!'

'No, you didn't enjoy it?'

'No, I meant that she didn't deserve it.'

'But you did bash her over the head, drag her into the woods and then strangle her to death.'

'No, I didn't!'

'You applied to be business manager but she got your job, the job you deserved, the job you craved.'

'That should have been my job. I'd worked there for years, I was older than her, more experienced, I knew how the university should be run. She changed everything. Experienced staff were made redundant or dismissed for no good reasons. She even made things up to get rid of staff and students. It was her together with Carlang and the Pro V-C.'

'Staff like Dr Elfyn Williams and Dr Bear Lawrence?'

'That was the final straw, neither of them had done anything wrong.'

'The final straw? Was it the mistreatment of those men that drove you to kill Charlee Butcher?'

'I didn't kill her!'

Both detectives went quiet and waited for the silence to be broken by Stacey Richards. When she failed to speak, DS Ash moved the timeline to after the murder. 'Did you know that trains are equipped with CCTV and they have a camera which records the drivers view in front of the train?'

'No, I didn't know that,' replied Stacey who looked a little nonplussed at the question.

'We have recordings from trains that were running about the time we're referring too. The various footage shows that Charlee Butcher's phone had to have been thrown onto the tracks, one hundred metres south of the Fallodon Hall railway crossing, shortly after she was murdered. We retrieved the phone and forensically examined it in detail.'

'I'm pleased for you, but I fail to see the relevance to me.'

DI Morter turned the laptop that was open and in front of him, around to face Stacey. The enhanced but grainy image of a woman in grey athletic clothing was on the screen. Both detectives watched closely to Stacey's reaction to seeing the image. She faltered only slightly, it was barely perceptible but definitely there. The silence hung in the air until it was broken by Stacey. 'Who am I supposed to be looking at?'

'That's you,' said DI Morter.

'No, it isn't, it could be anybody.'

'I'm afraid not. AI facial recognition algorithms have confirmed it is you.'

The two detectives let the room go quiet. DI Morter broke the silence and spoke more quietly than previously but with a firm tone.

'Charlee Butcher got the job you wanted, which you felt you deserved. To add insult to injury, she bossed the staff of HR about, including you. She was also instrumental in removing dedicated, experienced staff both in HR and throughout the university. Charlee Butcher made you wear a rainbow-coloured lanyard, the same type of lanyard that you used to kill her.'

'I didn't kill her.'

'The murder was premediated. You followed the route she ran twice on Monday evenings. You planned your escape route after the murder the following Monday. The next Monday you killed her with a rainbow lanyard after knocking her unconscious by bashing her head with a rock. Then you staged the murder scene to look like it had a sexual element by partially removing her clothing. But we found no evidence of a sexual assault or rape. You knew what phone Charlee Butcher used and you bought an identical one, which you swapped with hers after you murdered her. After fleeing the scene, you couldn't cross the railway tracks at the Fallodon crossing because a train was coming. Whilst you waited, you tried to get into Charlee's phone, but it was locked so you threw it onto the tracks.'

Nobody spoke for what felt to Stacey Richards like an eternity. The two detectives took in every piece of unspoken body language of Stacey Richards as she attempted to evade their piercing stares.

'You murdered Dr Carlang as well.' added DS Ash coolly.

Stacey looked down briefly as if trying to harden her resolve. 'Carlang died of a heart attack in hospital. He wasn't murdered. They said that on the news.'

'Stacey Richards, I'm arresting you for the murder of Dr John Carlang.'

'No, you can't! I didn't do it!' she pleaded.

DI Morter waded in. 'You poisoned his coffee with the medication prescribed for your husband and son. We have a forensic toxicology report of his Embleton United FC coaster. It matches their meds which you collected for them from the pharmacy.'

'I didn't, I didn't, I didn't!' Stacey was shaking her head and on the point of tears.

DI Morter turned the laptop back to face himself and began using the touchpad. When he had found what he was looking for, he turned the laptop back towards Stacey. It was playing an edited hospital CCTV recording.

'This is you walking towards and then entering the door leading to the Acute Cardiology Unit where Dr Carlang was. Notice you are carrying a bag. The footage now being shown is half an hour later. This is you leaving through the same door and without the bag. You poisoned Dr Carlang and murdered him.'

Stacey Richards could bare it no longer and started to cry. She bent over the desk and held her head in her hands, covering her face. Between the sound of her sobs, she spoke quietly, 'I'm sorry, I had to do it.'

'Do what?' asked DS Ash.

'I had to stop them.'

'By stop them, do you mean you killed them?'

'Yes.'

In the investigation room, Parrish punched the air.

Chapter 32 – Next time

That was the end of the interview for Parrish, but not for Stacey Richards. By Tuesday, she had explained everything, her remorse and her wish to be caught at the weight of guilt on her shoulders. She also admitted to her still lingering desire that Professor Vince Cook should get his comeuppance.

After logging out of the loaned laptop for the final time, Parrish left it on Mick's desk with a note. He had to go home to Helmsley to recuperate after first saying goodbye and thanking his friends Robbie and Christine for their hospitality.

On the following Thursday, a case of fine red wine was delivered to his cottage. Later the same day, a large bunch of flowers also turned up. Nobody quite knew whether Parrish was flying solo or had a partner. He was always very private on such matters. The flowers and wine came with thank you cards from Northumberland and Cheviots Police Force.

Hi Mick, thank you for the wine and flowers. When you have time, please give me a call, I'd like to hear how it all ended. Kind regards, P

The following day, Mick rang to thank Parrish. He debriefed Parrish on the interview and the usual battle with the CPS to get the case brought to court.

Thankfully, the confession of Stacey Richards was considered powerful enough backed by the evidence Parrish had contributed towards discovering.

'So, what about the case of Nataha Horseman?' asked Parrish.

'There is no case, it was suicide.'

'I read the confession of Devon Clarke and looked at the database, it just doesn't add up. Why did she not look at what the gulls were doing when she walked by them on her way to work? She deliberately told both Laura and Ian that she was going to look at the gulls. Ian was on the far side of the castle at the time and she had no reason to tell him having already spoken to Laura. Then she said she had vomited after seeing the image of the body on her phone. That's a quite extreme response.'

'It's also reasonable that some people will react like that though,' countered Mick.

'Yes, but I looked at all the video and photographic evidence in the database. There was no vomit. She made that up, she exaggerated her response.'

Mick sighed. 'I'm sorry Mr P, I've been ordered to let the coroner's verdict stand on this. Unless some new compelling evidence comes to light, this is going nowhere.'

The men wished each other well and hoped to see each other again sometime.

'Next time, I just might have that evidence,' said Parrish.

* * *

After the Dunstanburgh Castle business, Devon had been anxious and decidedly unsettled. The announcement in the news of the murder of Charlee Butcher had come as quite a shock to her, Embleton wasn't especially crime-ridden and murders were rare.

When she rationalised it, she decided that it was less likely that she would now get an unwelcome knock on the door with the police focused on The Butcher case. Consequently, as time went by, worries of what happened near Dunstanburgh Castle began to fade.

Devon was unaware of recent progress in the murder investigation. When an arrest was announced of a double murderer, nobody was more surprised than her.

For a time, this latest development unsettled her once again. But eventually she began to sleep more easily at night when that unwelcome knock on the door failed to come. One day, she might not rest so easy if Parrish had anything to do with it.

THE END

About the author

Dr Bear Lawrence is a former shop assistant, engineer, business owner, gardener, landlord, professional helicopter pilot, award-winning inventor, lecturer and racer of karts, yachts and motorbikes. He's had a very interesting life.

Suffering from stress as an overloaded university lecturer, he caught a viral infection and never recovered. Five months later he was diagnosed with Myalgic Encephalomyelitis (ME).

He now devotes his time and what energy he has to writing articles and books to raise awareness of chronic illnesses and hidden disabilities, plus his other interests.

He has planned a series of DCI Parrish crime thrillers and has started writing other novels in the series.

On Amazon you will find also some of his books in the 'Bear the Awarenessist' series.

me and my ME

Bear with ME

My School Bully

Bear in Mind

UnBearably Loud

Printed in Great Britain
by Amazon